The body was a sodden wreck, something even a lover would have trouble recognizing. The final burst from the gunman had flipped him over on his back. His shattered face was that of a man in his mid-twenties, with curly black hair and pale-blue eyes with long, feathery lashes. Beyond that, I couldn't even begin to guess.

The girl was where I'd left her. She watched my approach with the blank, expressionless stare of someone in shock. I bent down and pulled her gently to her feet. There was no resistance in her slender body and her hands were cold to the touch. *"Allons,"* I whispered, putting my arm around her.

Without speaking, she followed me out of the graveyard. . .

NICK CARTER
IS IT!

"Nick Carter out-Bonds James Bond."
—*Buffalo Evening News*

"Nick Carter is America's #1 espionage agent."
—*Variety*

"Nick Carter is razor-sharp suspense."
—*King Features*

"Nick Carter is extraordinarily big."
—*Bestsellers*

"Nick Carter has attracted an army of addicted readers . . . the books are fast, have plenty of action and just the right degree of sex . . . Nick Carter is the American James Bond, suave, sophisticated, a killer with both the ladies and the enemy."
—*The New York Times*

Dedicated to the Men of the Secret Services of the
United States of America

A Killmaster Spy Chiller

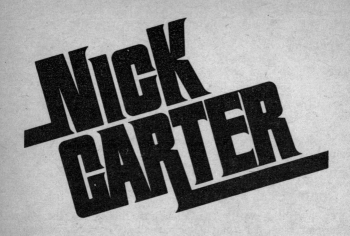

NICK CARTER

THE PARISIAN
AFFAIR

CHARTER
NEW YORK

A Division of Charter Communications Inc.
A GROSSET & DUNLAP COMPANY
51 Madison Avenue
New York, New York 10010

THE PARISIAN AFFAIR

An Ace Charter Original.

"Nick Carter: is a registered trademark of The Condé Nast Publications, Inc. registered in the United States Patent Office.

First Ace Charter Printing December 1981
Published simultaneously in Canada
Manufactured in the United States of America

2 4 6 8 0 9 7 5 3 1

THE PARISIAN AFFAIR

Chapter One

There's something about a graveyard, even one in a city as bright and bustling as Paris, that makes all your senses just a little more alert. The Cemetery Montparnasse was no exception.

It was on the Left Bank, a few blocks south of the famous Café Le Dome. Because of the well-known writers and composers buried there—Baudelaire, de Maupassant, Saint-Saëns, and Franck, to name a few—it did a brisk daytime tourist trade. But at an hour short of midnight, the place was cold, quiet, and deserted.

I'd been in the cemetery since ten, carefully checking and rechecking the grounds. It was a perfect spot for a set up. Almost too perfect. The maze of tombstones and vaults offered enough cover to hide a small army. For a single gunman, concealment would be child's play.

So far, the only thing I'd flushed out was a hungry-looking alley cat. But I still couldn't shake the feeling that I wasn't alone. And in my work, ignoring your gut instincts is the quickest way to wind up dead. I figured this place was crowded enough already; it really didn't need a stone marker engraved with the name Nick Carter.

There wasn't enough time left for another sweep of the grounds. The informant was due in ten minutes. I hunkered down behind a tombstone where I had a clear view of the main entrance on Boulevard Edgar-Quinet. Wilhelmina, my 9mm Luger, comfortably filled my hand.

Informants are a necessary part of the espionage business; even a super-secret agency like AXE employs a few. I never liked them very much and this one even less. He was an amateur and amateurs have an uncanny way of getting people killed.

Through an old friend of Hawk's, we'd put word out of a substantial reward for any information that could help us trace the assassin who had terminated four Third-World diplomats during the past two weeks. I'd gotten the call in my hotel room late in the afternoon. It was a man's voice, young, urgent, and strained with fear. "I have what Boissier says you want," he told me in heavily accented English. "Cemetery Montparnasse, eleven tonight—and don't forget the money."

The line went dead before I could say a word. It had all the makings of a set up, but I couldn't let it pass by. The anonymous, frightened voice was the only call I'd had after three days of impatient waiting. I had to go.

At exactly eleven, the cemetery gate eased cautiously open. Squatting in the wet grass, I watched a head appear and finally the slim figure of a man in a trench coat. I had assumed that this was going to be strictly one on one. But right behind the man was a blonde-haired girl, barely out of her teens.

I began to move toward them, staying low, using the shadow and cover of the headstones. There was no point in showing myself until I was closer. If this was an ambush, I'd need every advantage I could get.

After a moment's hesitation, the man started slowly up the graveled path with the girl trailing him a few feet back. His head darted from side to side like someone watching a tennis match. I think if I'd shouted "Boo" he would have jumped a good three feet into the air.

We were almost parallel now. I stepped out of the shadows and called out softly, "Over here."

Even that startled him a bit. But when he got a good look at me, his thin, pallid face flooded with relief. "Bon soir, Monsieur Carter," he said, grinning. "I was beginning to think you'd stood me up."

Gunfire split open the quiet night. The first shot hit him high in the chest, a dark circle of blood staining his trench coat. More slugs tore into the body, sending it jerking and spinning in a grotesque danse macabre. He hit the gravel face first, his arms spread wide in supplication.

The girl stood screaming, paralyzed with fear. I broke cover and tackled her as another burst of fire peppered my back with flying gravel. In a flurry of kicking legs, we rolled into the deep shadow of a family vault. I pushed her around the corner to safety and brought Wilhelmina into action.

It was no damn good. At that range a Luger is useless against a high-powered, semiautomatic rifle. The rifleman was on the top floor of a darkened building overlooking Rue Froideaux. From that vantage point almost the entire cemetery was in range. Thinking back now, I was glad that I'd trusted my instincts; the unseen presence I'd sensed hadn't been in the cemetery, but above it. Whoever planned the job was a real professional.

Bullets continued to pound the vault, pockmarking the limestone walls. I glanced back at the girl, who was making a low, moaning noise like keening at an Irish wake, her thin arms wrapped around her shivering body. It didn't look like she'd do anything dumb, like moving.

Belly down in the wet grass, I began to crawl toward the gunner's position, weaving in and out of the deep pools of shadow. If I could make the far wall, I would find a service entrance there that opened on to Rue Froideaux. I was getting tired of this duck shoot; once I reached the street it would be a two-way battle.

I was about twenty feet from the wall when the firepower shifted direction. I looked back and saw the body of the young man twisting spasmodically as the corpse took burst after burst of rapid fire. It was senseless and stupid, hatred in its ugliest form. The gunman was just too good not to know that he was already dead.

As suddenly as it had begun, the shooting

stopped. The cemetery was quiet again, but off in the distance I could hear the urgent, high-pitched wail of sirens. It was now or never, I thought, as I stood up and sprinted the short distance to the service entrance. I hit the street just in time to see a dusty, gray Citroën take the corner on two wheels. The deep-throated engine shifted into high gear as the car sped off into the night. Feeling frustrated and angry, I slipped Wilhelmina back into my shoulder holster. The killer was gone, but there was still plenty left for me to do.

The sound of sirens was louder now; I ran back into the graveyard.

The body was a sodden wreck, something even a lover would have trouble recognizing. The final burst from the gunman had flipped him over on his back. His shattered face was that of a man in his mid-twenties, with curly black hair and pale-blue eyes with long, feathery lashes. Beyond that, I couldn't even begin to guess.

Gingerly, I peeled back the blood-soaked trench coat and searched for his wallet. It was in his jacket breast pocket, miraculously intact despite the devastating barrage. But the contents were meager— just a few hundred francs, a driver's license in the name of Paul Julot, and a half-dozen business cards for a firm called Agency Castel. There wasn't enough time left for a thorough search of the body. I slipped the wallet in my pocket and then, almost as an afterthought, leaned over and closed his eyes.

The girl was where I'd left her. She watched my approach with the blank, expressionless stare of someone in shock. I bent down and pulled her gently to her feet. There was no resistance in her slender body and her hands were cold to the touch. *"Allons,"* I whispered, putting my arm around her.

Without speaking, she followed me out of the graveyard.

It was a *café tabac,* a small neighborhood place with a counter in the front and a back room with eight tables that served as the café. I sat the girl down at a corner table and ordered two double Remys at the zinc-topped bar. If the barman noticed the grass stains on my tweed jacket, he saw no reason to mention it. I left him a liberal *pourboire* and carried the glasses back to the table. There were only two other patrons, a pair of workmen in coveralls sharing a carafe of wine.

"Je m'appelle Nick Carter," I said, handing her the snifter of cognac. After what we'd been through, I figured it was about time we introduce ourselves.

"I speak English," she replied in a low, angry voice, "and I already know your name. Paul said it just before . . ." The words trailed off as she looked down at the table. "Who the hell are you?" she demanded, meeting my eyes again.

"I'm a reporter for the Amalgamated Press and Wire Services." I slipped my press card from my wallet and held it out to her.

"Don't play games," she said, pushing my hand aside. "Journalists don't carry guns and they don't get innocent people murdered." Her voice crackled a little as if the gory death scene were replaying itself in her mind.

In the light of the café she looked older than I had first guessed, early to mid-twenties. Her warm, honey blonde hair just touched the shoulders of her suede coat, framing a delicate oval face with a generous mouth and wide, sea green eyes. Her eyes were red-rimmed now and her face had the slackness that so often follows shock. In spite of all that, she was a very attractive woman.

"I'm sorry about your friend," I told her honestly. "There was nothing I could do. By the way, you still haven't told me your name."

"Lauren Savord," she said quietly. Then she began to cry. I let the jag run itself out, knowing she would feel better when she was done. After a few minutes her shoulders stopped moving and she raised her face away from her cupped hands. I handed her my handkerchief.

"I must look like *merde*," she said with a timid smile.

"Your eyes are a little dewy, but other than that, you look terrific."

"Liar," she said, laughing. "Can I have a cigarette, please?"

"Certainly." I offered her my case and lit one myself. "You were close to Julot?" I prompted.

"No, but it wasn't for lack of trying." She grinned ruefully and took a sip of Remy. "We both work at the Agency Castel; I'm a secretary and Paul handled some of the bookings. I've only been in Paris for two months. I come from Saint-Fiacre, a village near Matignon. It's so small you could drive through without ever realizing you were there. Maybe I arrived here with too many expectations. I thought I'd lead a different life in Paris, one filled with romantic evenings, walking arm in arm along the Seine and sharing intimate midnight suppers." She paused to blow a spiral of smoke toward the ceiling. "But it didn't work out that way. Tonight was my very first date. For weeks I'd been hoping Paul would notice me, at least say something more than 'Hello' or 'Get this letter out right away.' And finally, today he did."

"I find it hard to believe that it would take that long for any man to notice you."

Lauren tossed back her head and laughed. "Obviously, you don't know the Agency Castel, Monsieur Carter. It's one of the top modeling agencies in Paris, maybe in the world. The women who move through there every day aren't merely pretty, they're devastatingly beautiful."

"I suppose some of them move in the upper social circles? The arts and diplomatic scenes?" I tried to make the question sound casual, despite its importance.

"That's true," she responded quickly. "They're always being written up in the columns as having been seen at some premiere, gallery opening, or reception to honor a visiting head of state. It's only natural," she added with a typical Gallic shrug. "Powerful men like to be seen in the company of beautiful women."

I nodded silent agreement. This sounded as

though it might be the first real lead I had on the assassinations. All four victims had been high-ranking diplomats from Third World or emerging nations and in each instance they had been murdered in a high-security area, either the embassy itself or at a well-guarded, carefully screened reception. This was no amateur operation. Each one had been killed with swift, quiet precision—no mess, no commotion, just another dead body to add to the list. The methods varied: an air-filled hypodermic, curare poisoning, and in the last two cases, a simple knife across the throat. At three of the scenes, traces were found indicating the possibility that the assassin was a woman.

"You're suddenly very quiet," Lauren chided me.

"Just thinking. Tell me, weren't you surprised when Paul asked you out after all that time?"

"Well, I certainly didn't expect it," she said, grinning again. "He spoke to me about an hour before closing; he seemed nervous, jumpy, not like himself at all. He practically insisted I spend the evening with him. Of course, at the time I was very flattered, but all through dinner and the film we saw afterward, he kept looking at the people nearby as if he were afraid someone was watching him. It didn't do a whole lot for my ego."

"I could see where it wouldn't." I held out my cigarette case again, lit us both, and took a healthy sip of Remy. "What reason did he give you for going to the Cemetery Montparnasse?"

"Paul told me he had to meet a man about a

business matter. He said it would only take a few minutes and then we could go and have a nightcap at La Coupule. It sounded a little weird at the time, but I figured the way the evening was going what did I have to lose." Her wide eyes fixed me with startling intensity. "Why was Paul meeting you there?" she asked abruptly.

"In a way, it was a business matter," I admitted. "Julot had information to sell and I was the buyer. It's a common enough occurrence in journalism."

"What about murder? Is that common, too?"

"It happens. If I could have prevented it, I would have. I certainly didn't expect anything like that to happen."

Lauren finished the last of her cognac with a single, gulping swallow. "It wasn't as though we were close or anything," she said quietly, "but nobody should have to die that way."

My own thoughts were nowhere near as sympathetic. Maybe she hadn't realized it yet, but Julot had undoubtedly asked her out for a lot more than just the pleasure of her company. If the killer was someone they both knew, he had assumed he would be safer with a possible witness tagging along. Or perhaps he was one of those men who can't make a move without someone holding their hand. He had seemed scared enough to be the type. Whatever the reason, he had knowingly put an innocent woman in danger of her life. Let somebody else mourn the bastard.

"I'm going home now," said Lauren, pushing back her chair. We walked out together.

I found a cab rank a few blocks away on Boulevard Raspail. "Would you like me to see you home?" I asked.

She shook her head. "You seem awfully sure of yourself, Monsieur Carter. What makes you think I won't go straight to the police? Tell them I was there when it happened, give them your name?"

"You can if you want to," I said calmly. "But there wouldn't be much point to it. It won't change the fact that Julot's dead and there's nothing I can tell them that they don't already have from the evidence at the scene."

"You know," said Lauren smiling, "for no reason at all I trust you."

"I'm glad," I said truthfully. "I'll phone you tomorrow if you like."

"I'll be home: 47 Rue Mazarine. It's in the book."

I watched her taxi until it merged with the flow of northbound traffic. I'd considered grabbing the next cab in line and following her home, but it would only have been a waste of time. If the killer had wanted her dead she would have been back in the graveyard with Julot know.

I checked my watch. It was half past twelve, which would make it seven-thirty in Washington. Knowing my boss, David Hawk, he would still be at the office. I had a feeling he'd be pleased to hear that things were finally starting to happen.

Chapter Two

Number 19 Rue Froideaux was a turn-of-the-century luxury apartment building. It obviously had just been remodeled; the windows were all curtainless blanks and the tiny foyer smelled of fresh paint and plaster dust. If the police had been here at all, they were now long gone. My footsteps echoed sharply as I crossed the uncarpeted marble floor.

"Bon jour, Monsieur, a beautiful morning, no?" He popped out of the concierge's cubical like a child's spring-up toy, middle-aged and balding, with a white carnation in his buttonhole and the hearty smile of rental agents the world round.

"It's a fine day," I agreed. "I'm interested in an apartment on the top floor, something overlooking the street if it's available."

"I have only one left," he said eagerly. "Number 8, three bedrooms, two baths—and the view of Cemetery Montparnasse is superb."

"That sounds like exactly what I'm looking for."

"Good. Let me just lock up the office and I'll give you a tour."

"If it's all the same to you," I said quickly, "I'd prefer to look around on my own."

"As you wish, Monsieur." With a crestfallen expression, he slipped a key off a well-loaded ring and handed it to me.

"By the way," I said, "a friend of mine was supposed to stop by, late yesterday, to view the same apartment."

"La jeune fille, tres magnifique," responded the agent with a knowing leer. "You are indeed fortunate to have a friend of such beauty."

I returned his grin. "That certainly sounds like Christine. Tall, blonde hair and blue eyes?"

"Yes, she was tall, but as for the rest it was impossible to tell because of the hat and dark glasses."

"That was her, all right," I told him, heading for the elevator.

"It's the first door on your left," he called out after me.

As it turned out, I didn't need the key after all. The tall oak door opened at the touch of my hand. I eased Wilhelmina free of my shoulder holster and went in crouching low. The apartment was empty. I didn't bother with a room-to-room search, because the dusty parquet floor clearly revealed the passage of a single visitor in a trail that lead from the door to the balcony and back again.

The footprints were small, made by a woman's high-heel shoes. From the length of the stride she was five feet nine inches at least, probably taller. When describing my imaginary "friend" to the agent downstairs, I'd said "tall" for a specific reason. Height is one of the prime requirements of a fashion model. Being *tres magnifique* doesn't hurt, either. Every move I'd made so far seemed to bring me that much closer to the Agency Castel.

I stepped through French doors and out onto the balcony. It was small but sturdy, with a waist high wrought-iron railing in an elaborate floral design. I hunkered down and peered over the top. From a squatting position all but the very nearest part of the cemetery was within easy range of someone with a high-powered rifle. My eyes sought out the spot where Julot had died. In spite of an early morning rain, the gravel still retained the rust-brown color of blood.

There was no trace of her presence on the balcony floor, not a single cigarette butt or empty shell case. She'd probably waited there for hours— patient, motionless, poised for the kill. Gaining entrance would have been easy. Either she'd ducked back inside after she'd returned the key or simply returned later to pick the single, flimsy lock I'd seen on the lobby door. Although I didn't like the results in the least, I couldn't help admiring the handiwork.

The rental agent was waiting for me in the lobby. "Monsieur is impressed?" he asked, smiling.

"Very." I handed him back the key. "But I'd like to talk it over with my friend before I make a decision."

The Café Rénard Rouge never opens early.

It's a late-night spot, one of the favorite haunts of students, radicals, and people who break the law without ever making a living at it. Despite the often explosive mixture of crime and politics, it was a quiet, well-run café. The credit for that belonged entirely to André Boissier, *le rénard rouge* himself.

Although it was after eleven, I wasn't surprised to see the shutters still up and the outdoor tables and chairs stacked against the wall. I went up to the door and rapped on the glass.

"Fermé," a deep, rumbling voice called out.

I knocked again, louder.

"Cochon," the voice bellowed. The epithet was followed by slow, shuffling footsteps. Suddenly, an angry red face was peering out at me from behind the glass.

"Nick!" With recognition, the face broke into a wolfish grin. André Broissier opened the door, his red-rimmed eyes blinking at the sunlight.

"Good morning, André. I didn't wake you up, did I?"

"Of course not. Come in, Nick. I've just opened a new bottle of vintage calvados."

Boissier was a big man, six feet four and well over two hundred-and-fifty pounds. At sixty-three, his wavy red hair and full beard were flecked with gray, but his powerful arms and shoulders still looked as though they could squeeze the life out of a man without even trying. Drinking had aged him the most. His face had the pinkish, broken-veined flush of a heavy tippler.

He went behind the bar and poured calvados into two pony glasses, filling them to the rim. *"Bonne chance,"* he murmured, sliding my glass across the scarred walnut.

"Bonne chance," I replied. The tangy apple brandy had the warmth and kick of controlled fire. It was the best calvados I'd tasted in a long time.

Broissier finished his in one deep pull and wiped his beard with the back of his sleeve. "Too bad about Julot," he said quietly.

"I figured you would have heard about that by now."

The big man laughed. "More like an hour after it happened. He wasn't any great loss; a ladies' man, and from what I've heard, not even much in that department."

"Who gave him the word, André?"

Broissier shrugged. "A friend of a friend of a friend. I put it out just as Hawk requested. Julot was a regular here; he could have heard it from anyone of a dozen people." He paused and poured us both another shot. "Was he able to tell you anything before he died, *mon ami*?"

I shook my head. "We said hello and then the shooting started."

André laughed again and tossed back his brandy.

Like all men who've lived for long periods of time in constant fear for their lives. Broissier saw a certain grim humor in death. As a young man, he'd been a leader in the *maquis*, the French resistance movement. For three years he and his men had waged a hit-and-run war on the Germans occupying France. Seeming to be everywhere at once, they'd blown rail lines and arms depots, assassinated high-ranking Gestapo officers, and saved more than three hundred Jews and gypsies en route to the death camps. Because of his tactical brilliance and lightning speed he became known as *le rénard rouge*, the red fox.

I knew Boissier because of Hawk. He was one of three men I'd met who had the rare privilege of calling my boss by his first name. They went back a long way, to Hawk's very first assignment in the field. He was just twenty-four, as he liked to remind me, a raw Army recruit singled out to serve in the OSS by Wild Bill Donovan himself. After two months training, they dropped him in occupied France to operate as their liaison with the *maquis* south of Paris.

Hawk always ended the story there. Despite the close working relationship we'd developed over the years, I never felt I had the right to press him for details. Maybe some of it was still classified or maybe the retelling raised ghosts and memories better left undisturbed. I never asked and he never told me. The one thing that he did say was that he'd learned more "tradecraft" during these eighteen months spent with Boissier than he ever did during his long postwar run as an active agent, and that the burly Frenchman had saved his life twice. That alone was enough for me.

"Another drink, Nick?" André prompted.

"One more and then I've got to be going." I lit a

cigarette and started in on my third brandy. "There's something I'd like you to do for me, André."

"Name it," he responded eagerly.

"Spread the word around that my offer's still open, five thousand in gold Krugerrands for any information on the embassy killings."

"Money like that always brings someone out of the woodwork," he said, grinning. "It's only a matter of time. No operation can remain a secret very long without someone on the outside knowing about it."

I nodded silent agreement. As far as I knew, Boissier had never heard of AXE or of my own status as Killmaster N3. Through his long association with Hawk, he knew we were both in the "business," but that was as far as it went. He was a friend and a useful contact. Anything more would have jeopardized AXE security, not to mention my own life.

I said goodbye after promising to check in with him later that evening.

The sun was out in full force now, its warm glow burning off the chill in the November air. I decided to combine business with pleasure by asking Lauren to have lunch with me at Ledoyen on the Champs Élysées. I rang her number from a tobacconist's and got a busy signal. Forty-seven Rue Mazarine was less than ten minutes away. The walk would do me good.

She lived in one of those big, anonymous apartment complexes that have been springing up all over Paris since the early sixties. This one was all brick and glass, with tiny balconies and a parking garage below street level. I found Lauren's name opposite the bell for 2-B. In response to my ring, the lobby door clicked open and I walked in.

He leapt out of the shadows in a low crouch, a flaxen-haired man in a leather windbreaker. Light gleamed off the knife blade as he rushed me, the tip of the Bowie angled up for a single, gut-spilling slash at my unprotected abdomen.

I twisted aside and grabbed his knife arm. He was going so fast that the momentum carried him past me. I held on and twisted. He screamed as he hit the wall and the Bowie fell from his grasp, making a loud clanging noise on the tile floor.

I slipped Hugo into my hand and started toward him. His eyes widened at the sight of the stiletto. Noisily sucking in air, he scrambled for the knife just a few inches from his outstretched fingers.

I brought Hugo down in a flashing arc. He screamed again as the pencil-thin blade dug out a deep gash in his forearm. Blood gushed from the open wound, spattering his cheap leather jacket like a carelessly flicked paintbrush.

Rolling over, he kicked out at my groin. I pivoted and took the blow on my thigh. He was good, but running scared now. He tried to pull himself up, using the wall for support, but his eyes had that doomed look that says this is it, the end.

It was just as well that he didn't know I wanted information, not blood. I grabbed his shoulder and slammed him against the wall. We came face to face as I brought Hugo's tip to rest at the base of his throat.

"Who sent you?" I demanded. "Give me a name, just one name, and you can walk away from this."

"No." The single word came out in a harsh, sibilant whisper. Our eyes met for a second and then he snapped his head forward, burying Hugo in his throat halfway to the hilt.

I pulled the stiletto free and eased him down to the floor. Blood poured freely onto his chest. It was a hell of a way to commit suicide, fanatical and insane. If he could do this to himself, then what had he done to Lauren?

I took the stairs two at a time with Hugo in one hand and Wilhelmina in the other. The door to 2-B was ajar. I kicked it open and entered in a shooter's crouch, making my body as small a target as possible.

The room was empty.

In spite of the noisy entrance, there was no response of any kind. If Lauren was alive she would have cried out or tried to signal me in some way. Both the bedroom and kitchen were empty and undisturbed. Maybe she had decided to go into work after all, I kidded myself.

Her clothes were lying in a heap on the bathroom floor: a blue silk camisole and panties, nylons and a flower-print cotton dress. I leaned over and pushed back the shower curtain.

Lauren was in the tub, curled up on her side in the fetallike position of a sleeping infant. She was naked except for the twisted wire that had been used to bind her hands and feet. A towel had been shoved in her mouth to gag her.

As I reached down for it, her eyes flickered open, wild and bright, and very much alive.

Chapter Three

I lifted her up to a sitting position and eased the gag from her mouth. She sucked in air in hungry gulps, her body trembling from the effort. Her sea green eyes had the glassy, glazed-over look of someone suffering from a deep and traumatic shock.

"It's all right," I said softly. "I'm here and no one is going to hurt you now."

"I knew you'd come," she said in a hoarse whisper. "I didn't know how or why, but I knew you'd come."

She opened her mouth to say something more, but her eyes suddenly brimmed with tears and she dropped her head so that her honey blonde hair covered it like a mask.

Finally, she looked up again and met my gaze.

"Mon Dieu," she said in a barely audible voice. "He told me he was going to kill me. Exactly how he would do it and exactly what I was going to feel. He was holding that knife the whole time . . . cutting patterns in the air . . . as if I were already un-

der the blade. And when he looked at me . . . my body . . . it was always with the same, cold-eyed smile. It was horrible. I felt—" The rest of the words were choked off and lost in a long, plaintive sob.

I reached out and put a gentling hand on her shoulder. It was a simple reflex action—and it was also the wrong thing to do. I had no way of knowing. In shock cases like this, there just aren't any easy-to-follow rules.

At my touch, the sob turned into a silent scream and for a split-second her face was a twisted mask of agony. Then, mercifully, she blacked out. I managed to catch her head before it could hit the side of the tub. She was better off like this; a few hours of oblivion would go a long way toward healing the inner scars.

I lifted her up and backed my way out of the bathroom. The white porcelain, chrome fixtures, and gleaming tiles were beginning to remind me too much of a morgue. I had visited enough of them over the years—it comes with the territory. Some were newer and cleaner than others, but except for the tenants they were all basically the same —cold, brightly lit rooms that smelled of disinfectant and death.

Lauren's supple, long-legged body was light in my arms. I carried her into the living room and put her down on a high-backed green velour couch. Working quickly but gently, I loosened the twisted wire from her ankles and wrists, doing my very best to ignore the scent of her perfume and the way the sunlight made her skin glow like burnished gold.

Time was running out. And there was another body cooling rapidly in the lobby below. I wanted to get Lauren out of there before the *Sûreté* arrived. I'd watched them work on several occasions and after what Lauren had been through, they could very easily drive her over the edge. Maybe forever.

As if on cue, the piercing shrill of a *flic's* whistle cut through the steady flow of noise from the street. I slipped the last of the wire off Lauren's ankles and headed back to where I'd first found her.

The pile of clothes on the floor didn't offer much in the way of choices. The dress was one of those complicated affairs, all buttons, hooks and snaps; so it would have to be the camisole or nothing. The blue silk undergarment was just long enough to cover the vital parts, but the way it was cut wouldn't leave much to the imagination.

I slipped her limp arms through the straps, tugged the camisole down, and gathered her up in my arms again. The sounds from the street were more frantic now: orders being shouted, car doors slamming, boots thudding heavily against the pavement. The gendarmerie were quickly cordoning off the scene of the crime.

The tiny second floor landing was deserted. I jabbed the elevator button with my elbow, murmuring a silent prayer that the police hadn't already demobilized the car. Green lights flickered on the panel over the door as the car began a slow descent from three floors above. One good thing about these modern buildings is that they don't have the old-style European elevators—glass and steel cages that gave the passenger about as much privacy as a fish bowl.

Finally, the car reached two and the doors slid open. It was empty—our luck was running good. I stepped in and pressed the button marked G, holding it firmly down as we began to drop. If everything went according to plan, we'd have a quiet, uninterrupted trip down to the basement-level garage—uninterrupted in particular by a lobby full of gendarmes.

I took a deep breath as the green light on the overhead panel moved to L. The elevator stopped. The doors slid open.

"We'll catch this *découpeur* soon enough, Chief Inspector," said a soft voice with a thick provincial accent. "It has all the signs of a *Union Corse* killing, don't you agree?"

"Perhaps."

There were nearly a dozen cops in the lobby, uniform and plain-clothes, working in groups of two and three. The two men talking were only a few feet away from the open elevator doors. I could have reached out and touched them if I'd wanted to.

Instead, I continued to jab the button that would take us down to the basement. Just as the doors started closing, Lauren let out a low moan and began thrashing wildly, her bare feet pounding out a frantic tattoo on the car wall.

The pair by the elevator turned in unison. I caught a final glimpse of the man addressed as "Chief Inspector" just before the doors closed in his face. His expression was a mixture of bewilderment and rage.

Even more importantly, he had gotten a good look at me. The eye contact only lasted a split-second, but I had a feeling he would remember me all too well.

His subordinate's words were more comforting. Perhaps because the dead man also had been armed with a knife, he had quickly pegged the killing as the work of the *Union Corse,* the French equivalent of the Mafia. On the surface it did have the look of a grudge murder or gangland-style vendetta. I was the *découpeur* he had referred to— *découpeur* as in "carver of meat."

When the elevator doors parted on G level, I saw that our troubles were far from over. Two blue-caped gendarmes were guarding the entrance and exit ramps; one was stationed on the Rue Mazarine end and the other at the rear of the garage where the ramp led out to Rue Dauphine.

My only problem was how to neutralize them both at the same time. Even if I put Lauren down, the distance between the two cops still made it impossible. Of course I could have used Wilhelmina, but my fight wasn't with the French police. In this game they were little more than innocent bystanders.

There was only one solution. They would have to come to *me*.

"Au secours!" I yelled, walking out in plain view of both *flics*. "Mademoiselle is in immediate need of medical attention. You'd better take a look at her. I'm not even sure she's still breathing."

I'll never know for sure whether it was my call for help or the trim line of Lauren's bare legs, but both men deserted their posts at a brisk trot. The one from the Rue Dauphine end reached us first.

"What happened?" he asked, his eyes widening as he saw what Lauren was wearing.

"I don't know," I said. "We were coming down in the elevator together when all of a sudden she just passed out. I think she hit her head when she fell. You'd better take her, my arms are about to give out."

Before he could protest, I shoved Lauren into his arms.

"I'll call an ambulance," his partner said. He was standing just behind me, a little to the right.

I swung round and knocked him out with a light blow to the neck. As his legs buckled, I grabbed his collar and eased him down to the concrete floor.

"Son of a bitch," the first cop said in a stunned whisper. Short of dropping Lauren, there wasn't much else he could do. As he knelt to put her down, I snapped back his head with an open palm to the chin. When he woke up he'd have one hell of a headache, but no serious physical injuries. The whole thing took less than a minute, but I figured the Chief Inspector's men couldn't be far behind us.

The second car I checked had its keys in the ignition. I laid Lauren on the seat beside me and backed the small Renault out of its stall. Just as I began turning toward the Rue Dauphine exit, the stairwell door slammed open and half a dozen cops came spilling out, running with guns drawn.

I hit the clutch, shifted gears, and floored the gas pedal.

Chapter Four

Paris and New York are alike in many ways. One trait shared by the residents of both cities is a kind of wordly "we've-seen-it-all" attitude. Even the most outlandish dress or behavior rarely shocks them, and something that might draw a crowd in another city doesn't even rate a second glance from a native Parisian or New Yorker.

So I wasn't surprised by the reception we got when we entered the lobby of the Plaza Athénée. Lauren was still unconscious, but not as scantily dressed as before. I'd wrapped her up in an old army blanket I'd found on the back-seat floor of the Renault. It was frayed at the edges and it carried the smells of love-making and spilt wine. Lauren's long, tapered legs still dangled freely, but the rest of her body was enveloped in a scratchy wool cocoon.

"Bonjour, Monsieur Carter."

"Bonjour, Theo." The liveried attendant opened the door with a flourish, his eyes staring straight ahead at a point somewhere over my shoulder. I was a frequent guest and a generous tipper. I don't think Theo would have blinked an eye if I'd walked in carrying an M-16.

I crossed the luxurious circular lobby with Lauren in my arms. Except for an obvious pair of German tourists, no one so much as looked up from their newspapers or apéritifs. I stopped at the concierge's desk and was again greeted by name.

"Any messages?" I asked. I was expecting a call from Hawk with a cross-referenced list of names that I'd asked for when I'd phoned in my report last night.

"*Non*, Monsieur Carter. Is there anything else you require?"

"Not at the moment—although I may need the hotel physician later."

"You need only to phone me. Your key, Monsieur." He reached across the desk and laid it gently on top of the blanket. There wasn't much chance of it slipping off since the Plaza Athénée attaches each key to a large plastic medallion with the guest's name inscribed on the reverse side. It's a nice personal touch and it also allows the concierge to address each guest by name.

The service was one of many reasons why I always stayed in the Plaza Athénée when I had business in Paris. It is also one of the city's most beautiful hotels, with its arched windows and ornate balconies done in the palace-like style of pre-World War I architecture. Among the half-dozen great luxury hotels on the Right Bank, such as the

Georges V, Le Bristol, and Le Ritz, the Plaza Athénée has the best location. It's on Avenue Montaigne just off the Champs Elysées, only a block from the Rond Point and a few minutes walk from the Arc de Triomphe.

When I reached the small suite I had on the sixth floor, I stripped off Lauren's blanket and tucked her into my bed with the down-filled *édredon* to keep her warm. One side of me was all for waking her up. I urgently needed to know everything that had happened before I arrived on the scene. A name, a place, even a few words of political philosophy would help me to narrow the field. I did have the Agency Castel lead, but there was no telling how far that would take me.

As much as I wanted to, I still couldn't wake her. Last night she'd watched as the man beside her was cut down by a sniper and today her apartment had been invaded by a sadistic, knife-wielding maniac. That was one hell of a lot for any woman to handle, especially a nonagent who still didn't know why this was all happening. The best thing I could do for Lauren was to let her sleep her fill. I hoped she would wake up a rational, functioning human being. If she did go into shock, the hotel doctor could be with her in minutes.

There wasn't much else for me to do but wait for Lauren to wake up and for Hawk to phone with the information I'd requested. So I made myself a Chivas and water and carried it out to the balcony. My room overlooks the Avenue Montaigne, a pleasant, tree-lined street that houses numerous specialty shops and boutiques.

The midday sun was out in full force, cutting an intricate shadow pattern through the trees, its warm light somehow making all the passing women a little lovelier and more desirable than they really were. But then, that's Paris—magical in its way.

An hour and a half passed and I was just finishing my second drink when I heard Lauren thrashing around. I went in and found her tangled up in the *édredon*. Her wide, sea green eyes tracked me as I crossed the room.

"It's you," she said. Her face softened a bit and her eyes lost that fearful, haunted look. "Where am I?" she demanded. "And why am I here and—what in God's name is going on?"

"The first one is easy. You're in my room at the Plaza Athénée. There are several reasons for the 'why,' but mainly because it's the safest place for you to be right now. The rest of it is going to take some explaining and even then there certain things I can't tell you . . . things you'd be better off not knowing."

"Don't try and play games with me. I know you're an *espion*—that press card is just a CIA cover."

Espion, the French word for spy. Someone knew I was an intelligence agent, but they *didn't* know who I worked for. Very interesting.

"Did the man with the knife say I was CIA?"

Lauren nodded. "He even knew your name and what you looked like. He said you were working against France, trying to undermine our government and economic stability."

"I guess he told you all this before he started in with the Bowie knife?"

"Oui." She trembled slightly and pulled the *édredon* around her as if the room had suddenly grown cold.

I offered her a cigarette, took one myself, and lit them both. "Listen," I said sitting down on the edge of the bed, "you have to trust someone, Lauren. I didn't get you involved in this, your friend Julot did. Apart from the fact that I always like meeting a beautiful woman, I really wish you'd never walked into that graveyard. But you did and now I need your help . . . France needs your help, too."

"How do I know that what that man said isn't true?"

"You just have to trust me," I said. "It might help if you forgot about the accusations for a minute and remembered what *they* did to Julot and what they threatened to do to you. It doesn't exactly add up to this country's motto—*Liberté . . . Egalité . . . Fraternité.*"

"That's true," she admitted. "But I still can't understand why you ran away from the gendarmes last night."

"Let's just say I am here on government business. If we'd waited around for the police, they'd want to question us both. I don't know if you've ever had any dealings with the *flics*, but they have a neat little law here called *garde-à-vue*. It means they can hold you for twenty-four hours for no reason at all, forty-eight if they think the case involves national security. I couldn't risk letting that happen. There's too much at stake."

Lauren gave me a slow, hesitant smile. "All right, you've convinced me. At least for the moment," she quickly added.

"Fine. Now if you're feeling up to it, I'd like you to tell me everything that's happened to you since I put you in the cab last night."

"First, another cigarette, please."

I gave her one and watched as she pushed the pillows back and made herself comfortable.

"When I got home," she began, "I checked to make sure all the windows were locked and put the night-chain on the door. I felt like I wanted to sleep for a week, but I made myself take a bath first. I don't think I had any blood on me, but I just didn't feel *clean*. Then I slept, woke up around ten, and made myself café au lait. The man came a little after eleven."

"Came how?" I asked. "Did he break in or did you open the door for him?"

"I let him in," she said meekly. "He told me he was with the CRS, the national security police, and that he wanted to question me about Julot's murder."

"Did he question you about it?"

"No," she said looking away from me. "I feel like such an *imbecile*."

"Don't," I said softly. "We've all been there before. Besides, you had no way of knowing."

"Well, there was something strange," she said,

meeting my eyes again. "He didn't seem interested in what happened in the cemetery. It was almost as if he already knew all about it. He just kept asking me about what happened *before*. 'Did Paul speak to anyone after we left work? Did he say anything odd or out of place during the course of the evening? Did he give you any message or object to pass on to M'sieur Carter?' He went on like that for nearly half an hour. Always the same questions, just phrased a little bit differently each time."

"Let's go back to the beginning," I suggested. "Did he give you his name? Show you any identification?"

"Dossin," Lauren said quickly. "No first name. He did flash a small leather card case under my nose. But he only held it open for a second; it could have contained an old *Métro* ticket for all I know."

"This next question is important, Lauren. Judging from his accent, his mannerisms, where would you say he was from?"

"France," she replied without hesitation. "Not Paris, but somewhere in the south. Maybe Gascogne or Auvergne."

"That's important information," I said encouragingly. She seemed more confident now, but there was a distant quality to her voice as if she were describing a movie she'd seen or some incident that happened long ago. Sooner or later she would have to come to grips with the fact that it had happened to *her*.

"Now let's go back to where we left off," I said.

"What other questions did he ask?"

"He wanted to know about my relationship with Paul. Like how often we went out and how many times had we slept together. That's when I really started getting nervous. What could that possibly have to do with his murder?"

"Nothing," I said. At least nothing that I knew about so far.

"I wanted to get away from him for a minute, to phone the police and find out if he really was with the CRS. My phone is in the kitchen. I suggested café and he said that sounded fine."

She paused for a moment and took a deep breath. "He followed me. I didn't even know he was there until I felt his hand slipping around my waist. I screamed and struggled, but he was just too big. He carried me into the bathroom, stripped me, and tied me up with some wire coat hangers he found there."

"Was that when he started telling you that I was a foreign agent working against France?"

She nodded and turned her head away.

"Then what happened?"

"I don't want to talk about it," Lauren yelled. She pointed a finger at me, her eyes bright with anger. "Questions, questions, why don't you answer some for a change?"

"Fair enough. What do you want to know?"

"Where are my clothes?" she asked, pushing back the *édredon*. "What I've got on is fine for your bedroom, but I don't quite think I can walk out of the hotel like this."

"The rest of your things are still at your apartment. We had to leave in a hurry; the best I could come up with was that blanket." I pointed to the floor where it lay in a tangled heap. "The Christian Dior boutique is just down the street. You can call them through the front desk, order whatever you want, and they'll add it to my hotel bill."

"Then I'm free to go?"

"It isn't as simple as that. It wouldn't be safe for you to go back to your apartment, not for a while yet. I could arrange to put you in a safe house here in Paris, or else, if you'd like to take a vacation I could . . ."

"You lied to me," Lauren screamed. "You told me he was dead, you bastard."

I grabbed her arm, pulling her close to me. "He is dead, Lauren. If you still don't believe me, you can read about it in tonight's papers. *France Soir* will be on the stands in just a few hours."

"I don't know what to believe anymore," she whispered. She began to cry; her head resting on my shoulder. I took her in my arms, holding her trembling body tight against mine. I rocked her gently, almost as I would a child, and the sobbing gradually diminished to a whimper.

Lauren raised her head and with her eyes still closed, sought out my mouth. Her generous lips were warm and soft as she kissed me with the kind of desperate hunger that comes from being close to death. Her body began to move slowly, her breasts brushing across my chest in a smooth rhythmic motion.

I eased her back and slipped the camisole off. Some women reach their peak in their teens, but Lauren had blossomed later. Her lightly tanned skin was flawlessly smooth and full breasts were firm and upright, their dark circular nipples erect.

As we continued to kiss and caress, her hands eagerly undid my shirt and belt. I slipped out of my clothes and lay down beside her. We took our time, each of us exploring the other, touching, feeling, building the fire.

She moaned softly as I entered her, her long legs riding my back while she held me close. At first the love-making was a frantic reaffirmation of life, but gradually we moved into the intimate rhythms of pleasure. I'm still not sure how long we stayed together, except that when we finally stopped, night had already begun to darken the Paris skyline.

Chapter Five

"Christine Dalton, Ann-Marie Michaels, and Gail Huntington," Hawk said, reading down the list. "The first two are French nationals and the last one is an American expatriate. All three of them are high fashion models working for the Agency Castel—and all three of them attended the receptions at which a diplomat was terminated."

As usual, he was precise and to the point. Hawk's voice had the clear, metallic quality to it that we always get whenever we're using the scrambler on both ends. His call had come a few minutes after eight, just as Lauren and I were finishing up a room service supper of veal, *profiteroles,* and a bottle of *Puligny-Montrachet.* Through the half-open door I could see her head in profile, the lamplight shining on her honey gold hair.

"That does tend to back up your Castel theory," he went on, "but running the guest lists through the computer also shows us that there were eighty-seven *other* people who attended all of the receptions. I'm sure you already realize this isn't a matter of coincidence. Almost all of these people were diplomats who accepted the invitations because it was part of their job. It would have been an insult, a breach of protocol not to."

"What about the other nondiplomats?" I asked.

"Alex Raymond, the newspaper columnist, and his wife, and Gail Huntington's escort, Carlos Ramez. He's an importer with offices in Paris and Bogota. His uncle is cultural attaché to the Colombian Embassy in Paris." Hawk paused, and I heard the metallic click of a lighter as he fired up one of the foul-smelling cigars he was constantly smoking. "I'm sending all the information we have by courier," he continued, "but as far as the three models are concerned, it amounts to practically nothing."

"I can take care of that on this end, sir."

"I'm sure you can, Nick. That isn't what worries me. Our biggest problem is the upcoming Arab oil summit. It's due to start in three days and in spite of the diplomatic pressure both from France and ourselves, the Arabs flatly reject the idea of postponing it or relocating somewhere other than Paris. The Arabs are a logical target for this kind of terrorist group and we both know what the consequences could be if they were successful."

The implications were so enormous that even Hawk hesitated in speaking about them on a secured line. Still, I knew exactly what he meant. The Middle East was already a tinderbox, needing only the smallest spark to set it ablaze. An assassination would do just that. Hostile neighboring states would jump at the chance to wage war on one another. The world's oil supply would be drastically reduced almost overnight, pulling the superpowers into the conflict whether they wanted to be involved or not. What Hawk didn't want to talk about was global confrontation—in short, a Third World War.

"Is there anything else, sir?" I asked.

"Just one other thing, Nick. I've arranged for you to attend a reception at the Somalian consulate tomorrow evening. All of the suspects are also on the guest list. It should give you a chance to look them over in their natural habitat. I'm sure you won't have any problem finding a suitable young lady to take along."

"I don't think so, sir." We both said good night and when the line went dead, I unhooked the portable scrambler, packing away its miniaturized components inside the frame of the typewriter I carried as part of my journalistic cover.

"You were a long time on the phone," Lauren said when I walked back into the room. "I was starting to think you were neglecting me," she added, her tone of voice half-flippant, half-serious. "Possibly my new outfit will make you think twice about that."

She rose from her chair and did a slow, full-circle turn for my inspection. She did look *fantastique*. Her call to Dior had produced a wine-colored silk blouse, tan suede trousers that fit her like a second skin, and a pair of high-heeled, dark-brown

Western boots. I knew the bill would cause a few ripples when it reached the AXE accounting department, but it was worth it. Lauren not only looked different now, but her whole attitude had changed since this afternoon's love-making. Her shaking and mood-swings had stopped; now she smiled often and had even laughed twice during dinner. I knew she still wasn't over the shock of the last two days and that she probably never would be. The horrors were buried somewhere just below the surface and sooner or later, they would rise again to haunt her.

"You look terrific," I told her.

"Merci, Monsieur. Now that I'm so beautifully turned out, the least you can do is take me out for the evening. A new form of what you call 'protective custody,' " she added with a wide, provocative smile.

"I'm sorry, Lauren, but I have something very important to take care of. Something that just can't wait. I'll make arrangements for someone to stay here with you until I get back; I shouldn't be gone more than a few hours."

"No," she said with quiet force. Having spoken that single word, her full lips formed a hard, stubborn line while her sea-colored eyes stared back at me defiantly. "Either I'm going with you," she continued, "or I'm going home—where I'm sure the gendarmes still have somebody waiting for me. I know you wouldn't have any problem stopping me, but I'll try just the same. I just don't think I could stand being left alone tonight, and I'm not

42

talking about some goon you'll bring in to keep me company. Please, Nick," she said more softly, "take me with you."

In a way, I should have seen it coming. After what she'd been through it was only natural that I would become someone to cling to, someone she wouldn't want to let go of too soon. That's the trouble with my business—no time and no emotion allowed for personal relationships.

Tonight's job was an easy one with not much risk involved. Since we had so little on the three models, I'd decided to break into the Agency Castel for a look at their files. Along with the basic background information, they were also likely to contain lists of their recent bookings, including who had employed them and what foreign countries they had visited for photo sessions. The profession was a perfect cover for an agent or courier. And the files might help me tie one or all of them to the terrorist assassinations.

I could take Lauren with me. Since she worked for the agency, her knowledge of the layout would be helpful. As far as keeping her protected went, she might be better off with me. It went against everything in the rule book, but then I'd never really followed it anyway.

I turned away, heading for the other room where I could strap on Wilhelmina, Hugo, and Pierre in privacy. "I hope that outfit comes with a jacket," I called back over my shoulder, "because it looks like we're in for some rain."

Chapter Six

It was pouring by the time we reached our destination. The modeling agency was located on the Avenue Elysée Reclus in a corner building overlooking the carefully groomed gardens of the Champ de Mars. The building itself was a turn-of-the-century private residence with a limestone façade and heavy, cast-iron grill work covering the street-level windows. Lauren had told me that the agency occupied all four floors; she knew that they didn't employ a night watchman and she didn't *think* that the place was rigged with an alarm system. But then, we'd be finding out the answer to that one soon enough.

Lauren and I were standing in a doorway on the other side of the avenue. With our arms around each other, we looked like two typical Parisian lovers who didn't give a damn about the weather. I held her so that I had a clear, unobstructed view of the agency. In the twenty minutes that had passed since our arrival, the windows had remained dark and no one had either come or gone through the arched double doors that formed the main entrance.

"This is nice," Lauren whispered, "but can't we go in now? I'm starting to get cold."

"In another minute," I said, suppressing an urge to laugh. I don't think this was quite the evening out she'd expected. I drew her closer to me, softly stroking the back of her neck. She'd shown no surprise when I'd told her that we were going to be breaking into her employer's offices. In fact, she'd said it sounded like fun.

Traffic on the avenue was light. I watched as a battered green Citroën passed by, the twin headlights dimmed by the wind-swept rain. When I heard it turning onto Rue Harispe, I decided that now was as good a time as any.

"Allons," I said quietly. "If we don't run you're going to get drenched. But watch your step; I don't want you twisting an ankle. We may have some real running to do on the way out."

Lauren slipped her arm through mine and with our heads down we sprinted across the rain-slick cobblestones. The next part was the hardest. For at least a minute, we would be silhouetted by the overhead light, with no way of hiding from the *flics* who frequently cruised the area in their small black-and-white Renaults.

"Stand in front of me," I told Lauren, "facing the street as if you were waiting for someone." There were no traces of an alarm system on either the door or the frame. With my set of picks in hand, I knelt down behind Lauren and began to probe the lock. It was nothing special, a standard cylinder arrangement that any amateur could have opened with a few hours of training. I slipped in another pick, gave it a slight turn, and heard the metallic click of the tumblers falling into place. The door eased open at the touch of my hand.

"Let's get inside," I said, pushing Lauren in ahead of me. I slid in behind her, relocked the door, and took out the pen-sized flashlight I'd brought along.

The building may have been old, but inside the place was ultramodern. I played the narrow beam of light over the reception area, illuminating a glass-and-chrome desk, matching chairs, and an abstract bronze sculpture nearly as tall as I was. Except for a small table stacked with fashion magazines, there was nothing to indicate that this was one of the top modeling agencies in the business.

"This is just to impress the clients," Lauren said as though she had read my thoughts. "The real work takes place upstairs. That's where the files are, too, on the second floor."

"Fine, we'll take the stairs; elevators make too much noise. And stay a few feet behind me on the way up—we're still not sure there isn't anyone else in the building."

The staircase was narrow and winding. I turned off the flashlight and we made our way up slowly, staying close to the wall in case we hit a creaky tread. When we reached the top, I paused and surveyed the shadow-filled room.

"Okay," I said, flicking the flashlight back on.

"Show me where the files are."

Lauren took my hand and led me past a long row of desks. Unlike the reception area, there were pictures everywhere—some framed, some merely tacked up on corkboard. Caught for a second in the flashlight's beam, they seemed to smile back at me—poised, beautiful and seductive.

"This is the file room," Lauren said, leading me through a doorway. "There aren't any windows, so if you want to shut the door, I can put on the light."

"Go ahead," I told her. Lauren flicked the switch and I blinked my eyes to readjust them to the glare from the overhead neon florescent lighting. The small room contained nothing but three walls of gray-metal filing cabinets, a scarred oak table, and two chairs. None of the file drawers were locked, so it took me little more than a minute to locate the three folders I wanted.

"Who are they?" asked Lauren, peering over my shoulder.

"Just some women I'm interested in."

"Bulle merde," she said with a quiet laugh.

But I was interested in the three photographs spread out on the table before me. They were portrait shots, in black and white, and the only word to describe them was stunning. Each of the women was incredibly beautiful in a different way; together, they were almost too perfect to be real. Christine Dalton, Gail Huntington, and Ann-Marie Michaels . . . as difficult as it was to accept, one of them was probably a ruthless, cold-blooded professional assassin.

I thumbed through the thick pile of papers behind each picture. There were assignment sheets, medical histories, biographies, and press clippings. Just about everything I would need for a complete background check.

"Nick, can we get out of here?" Lauren asked, tugging at my sleeve. "If I don't get out of these wet clothes, I think I'm going to catch pneumonia."

"Just a few more minutes," I promised. "I want to make copies of these and return the originals to the files." I was tempted to remind her that she had insisted on coming along, but I decided to let it pass.

"There's a Xerox machine down the hall. You might as well let me make the copies—God knows I've had enough practice."

The big copier made a quiet humming noise that was barely audible unless you were standing by it. Lauren fed the photos and papers in while I held the flashlight and we soon had full copies of all three folders. I slipped the whole packet into an envelope I'd brought along and tucked it under my belt. If we did run into anyone, I wanted to have my hands free.

We quickly replaced the originals and began to thread our way through the desks, back toward the stairs. It was then that I heard it—the sound of footsteps almost masked by the hard, drumming noise the rain made on the windows.

"Down," I whispered, pulling Lauren to the

floor. We were behind a big metal desk with the rear wall of the building just a few feet in back of us. The stairs and elevator were both on the other side of the room, so our location made an ideal observation point with a fairly small risk of being discovered. Of course, I wasn't taking any chances. I'd already drawn Wilhelmina; the 9mm Luger felt cool and comfortable in my hand.

The footsteps grew louder as they reached the top of the stairs. There were two people coming up, one heavy-footed, the other light. I peered over the desk just as they reached the top. In the darkness they were nothing more than vague, shadowy forms.

"Turn on a light," a deep, gutteral voice demanded. "I'll be damned if I'm going to break a leg tripping over all this crap." The words were harsh and forceful, with just the slightest trace of a Spanish accent.

"Okay, you don't have to shout," a woman answered.

I heard a click and one of the desk lamps came on, casting a pale cone of light on the two figures. One of them I knew and one of them I didn't.

The man was squat and powerfully built, with broad-shoulders and a barrel-chest. His face was squarish and craggy, featuring thick brows, a broken nose, and a drooping moustache that didn't quite hide the hard set of his mouth. In the lamplight his face looked like the crudely carved stone head of an Aztec deity—one of their many cruel and uncompromising blood-gods. He was wearing a rumpled gray suit and a heavy overcoat, the front of which was stained with cigarette ash. The pink rosebud pinned to his lapel was withered and brown at the edges.

"Let's get on with it, bitch. I don't have all night."

"Sure, Hector, whatever you say."

I'd recognized the woman he'd called "bitch" as soon as the light went on. It wasn't difficult, considering that I'd been looking at her picture only a few minutes earlier. Gail Huntington looked even better in person. The black-and-white photo couldn't capture the warm chestnut color of her shoulder-length hair or the depth of her luminous green eyes. It also didn't hurt that she had a figure that would make *any* man stop and stare. The blue jumpsuit she was wearing hugged the contours of her body like a second skin. Now I could see why Lauren had developed an inferiority complex working there.

I watched as the American model leaned over one of the desks and detached a plastic-wrapped bag tapped beneath it. She carried it over to the man called "Hector," holding it out in front of her at arm's length. I had a feeling that she didn't want any physical contact with him.

"The weight feels right," he said, hefting the bag with one hand. "I don't think you'd be stupid enough to try and short me. You wouldn't look nearly so pretty after they fished your bloated body out of the Seine. *Comprendo?*"

"I'd never do anything like that," she said quickly. Her voice was dry-throated and crackling with fear.

"How reassuring," Hector said, grinning. "As long as you remember that, we won't have any problems. Because I settle them all the same way— swiftly and eternally."

The hand he'd kept in his overcoat pocket came out holding a gun. It was a German-made Sauer-Selbsladepistole, a 7.65mm automatic that they'd stopped making after the war. He held it low and to the side, not quite pointing at her. Still, he only needed to move it a few inches for a perfect stomach shot.

"Can't you put that away?" she asked meekly. "Please, Hector."

He smiled, exposing uneven teeth stained with nicotine. "It makes you nervous, no? I like it when people are nervous, they listen better that way. Now I want you to pay close attention to what I'm going to say."

She nodded silently, her eyes never leaving the gun.

"The rendezvous I told you about before is definite now. The consul is anxious to meet you and it's going to be big. A real killing, unless you screw it up."

"I won't, Hector. I promise you everything will be perfect."

"It had better be. Now get going. When I leave here in five minutes, I want you to be halfway home."

Without speaking she headed for the stairs,

pausing only once for a quick, frightened glance over her shoulder. I listened as the sound of her footsteps faded into silence.

Hector put the plastic bag down and lit a cigarette. His other hand was still loosely gripped around the vintage automatic.

I slipped my arm around Lauren and pulled her close. She'd been shivering ever since we'd crouched down behind the desk. Whether it was from her wet clothes or Hector's presence, I couldn't be sure. Most likely, it was a combination of both.

When five minutes had passed, Hector ground out his second cigarette on the desk top and slipped the package into his overcoat pocket. He took a slow, careful look around the room and then switched off the light. Lauren and I listened to his heavy tread on the stairs and then, a few seconds later, the sound of the street door closing.

I helped Lauren up and tucked Wilhelmina back into my shoulder holster.

"What an evil man," she said in a hushed voice. "Have you ever seen him before?"

She shook her head. "He isn't someone you're likely to forget."

When we reached the street I saw his broad back about a block and a half ahead of us. He was headed south, walking at a leisurely pace in spite of the rain. We closed the distance to a couple of hundred feet and followed him for three blocks until he entered an apartment building on Rue de Belgrade.

Standing in the shadows, I watched the lights go on in the third-floor front apartment. It was a pretty good guess that our friend Hector was home for the night.

"I'm freezing," Lauren complained. "Can we go back to the hotel now, Nick?"

"I have to make a phone call first, but there's a café down there on the other side of the street. I think we both could use a double Remy to fight off the chill."

It was near closing time and the café was almost empty. The man behind the *zinc* poured us generous doubles and gave me a *jeton* for the phone. While I made my call, Lauren pulled up a chair next to the big pot-bellied stove that heated the place. When I looked back over my shoulder, I saw she was smiling again.

"This is N3," I said after I'd exchanged the recognition code with the woman who answered. "I want round-the-clock surveillance, effective immediately, on number 16 Rue de Belgrade and number 20 Avenue Gabriel." I went on to describe Hector and Gail Huntington, and told the field-office operator that under no circumstances were the agents to come in contact with the two subjects.

I hung up the phone and sat there for a moment. Our trip to the agency had turned up more than I expected, but it also gave me some *new* questions to find the answers to. Like, who was Hector and what were he and the American model up to? And what did the bag contain—narcotics, explosives, or something else? Three words that Hector had spoken kept running through my mind—"rendezvous, consul, killing." Maybe I'd already found my assassin.

Chapter Seven

The bedside phone rang a few minutes after nine. I picked it up quickly before the noise could waken the tousle-haired figure lying next to me.

"*Allô.*"

"*Bon jour,* M'sieur Carter. This is the concierge speaking. I hope I didn't disturb you, but you asked to be informed the moment your car arrived. I'm happy to say it's here. I took the liberty of having your driver put it in our garage. If you like, I can send the keys up to your room."

"Thanks, but I'll be coming down in about fifteen minutes. Don't bother to have the attendant bring it around. I'd rather take care of that myself."

"Whatever you wish, M'sieur Carter."

I was glad to hear it had finally arrived. When Hawk had ordered me to Paris, I'd had to leave the Ferrari 512 Boxer down in Naples and take the first available flight. Before I'd left, I'd made arrangements with Dave Harris, an old friend and ex-North American Racing Team engineer, to drive the car up for me. It was a favor he'd been more than willing to do. When I'd bought the twelve-cylinder Ferrari, I'd let him spend a few hours behind the wheel. It was a classic case of love at first sight. Even though we were good friends, I wasn't surprised that he hadn't waited to say hello. There was probably some car he wanted to look at here in Paris. Dave had always related better to cars than to people.

"Morning," Lauren said in a soft, sleepy voice.

"Good morning. I've got to go out for awhile. Why don't you sleep in?"

"Excellent idea," she muttered, smiling at me with half-closed eyes. She sighed once and rolled over on her stomach, her long legs kicking back the covers.

I knew I was beginning to care too much for this lovely and vulnerable woman. It was an occupational hazard that comes from too many nights spent in dark doorways and too many face-to-face meetings with sudden death. God knows, I'd had more than my share of women—beautiful, exotic, and talented women. But there was something special about Lauren. I didn't look forward to the day when it would have to come to an end.

After I'd showered, shaved, and dressed, I had just enough time left to gulp down a cup of room service coffee. Neither Bellows nor Monroe, the field agents in charge of the surveillance teams, had phoned in yet, which meant that nothing out of the ordinary had taken place. Still, I was anxious to be there myself. And I'd decided the Huntington stakeout would be first on my list.

Her file had made for some very interesting reading. First, there was her background. According to her personal data sheet, her mother had died in childbirth and she'd been raised single-handedly by her father, Sergeant Vincent Huntington, an Army weaponry instructor. She'd participated in numerous rifle and handgun competitions, and had won nearly a dozen trophies by the time she was seventeen.

The other thing that had caught my eye was of a rather different nature. Written at the top of her employment record in thick block letters were the words: "Refuses to work with blacks of any nationality." The single word "blacks" had been underlined three times for emphasis.

The marksmanship and the racism fit in perfectly with the profile I'd been developing of our unknown assassin. Add the scene I'd witnessed last night and it made an even stronger case against her. I certainly wasn't eliminating Christine Calton and Ann-Marie Michaels yet, but Gail Huntington was far and away my leading candidate.

I spotted the Ferrari the moment I walked through the garage door. Harris had backed it into a corner slot where it was less likely to get clipped by a careless driver. The 512 is a sleek and graceful two-seater with a low roof and a steeply slanting windshield and hood. Mine was British racing green in color. The car was too conspicuous to use for tailing jobs, but unparalleled when it came to precision driving and speed. It could go from zero to seventy in 6.8 seconds with a top speed of one hundred and sixty-four mph.

I eased it out into the flow of traffic and headed north on Avenue Montaigne. Like Rome, Paris is one of those cities where drivers are not noted for their courteous attitude toward pedestrians. They prefer flicking their brights to using their brakes. It sometimes makes crossing the street a real test of your running ability.

I crossed the Champs Élysées through the Rond Point and turned right on the Avenue Gabriel. Number 20, where Gail Huntington lived, was a small but well-kept building with a *porte cochère* gateway and a cobblestone courtyard in front. I drove by slowly but didn't stop. In my rearview mirror I caught a glimpse of Steve Woodriss, an AXE field operative attached to the Paris office. He was sitting in a blue Renault parked directly across from the building. If he'd seen me, he did nothing to acknowledge it. I drove two more blocks down Gabriel and parked the car opposite the British Embassy.

"Nick, old boy. They told me you'd be dropping by. How are you?"

"Fine, Steve," I said, sliding into the front seat. "How about yourself?"

"Couldn't be better, thank you. The American girl took off half an hour ago with Monroe tailing her. Left me here to keep an eye on the place."

"Any activity?"

"No, it's been as quiet as a country churchyard."

Some people think that vodka doesn't have any

odor, but Woodriss literally reeked of it. I'd caught the full power of his sour breath when he'd turned to answer my questions. On the seat beside him was a brown paper bag just about the right size and shape to hold a pint.

"Care for a nip?" he asked when he saw me looking at it. "I know it's against the regs," he added quickly, "but I've got to have *something* to keep the old circulation going."

"No thanks, Steve."

"Suit yourself," he said, turning his red-rimmed eyes back to the building.

It's never pleasant to watch someone falling apart. Woodriss had been a good agent once; not Killmaster level, but a solid and capable field man. That was before the Khmer Rouge got hold of him back in '75. He'd been heading out of Cambodia with important information about troop movements in the interior. When we'd finally gotten him out two months later, there wasn't a whole lot left of the man we'd known. The physical scars eventually healed, but time didn't seem to help what the Khmer Rouge had done to his mind.

AXE always takes care of its own. Hawk gave him a desk job in Paris when he was well enough to go back to work. He'd been there ever since then, shuffling papers and gradually drinking more and more. He could still handle the daily routine, but they rarely sent him out on even a simple surveillance assignment unless they were understaffed.

"Cigarette?" Woodriss offered, holding out a pack of Craven A. I would have preferred my own custom brand, but I took one just the same. He already felt bad enough that I'd caught him drinking; there was no need to make him feel worse.

His hand trembling slightly, he lit us both, and tossed the match out the window. The cigarettes were only one of the British mannerisms he had. Other more obvious ones were his neatly trimmed "regimental" mustache and the Harris tweed sports coats he wore year round. Actually, he was Anglo-American, since his mother was from London and his father from Baltimore. He'd gone to one of the better English schools and always took a great deal of pride in wearing the school tie. If he hadn't been recruited by AXE, it could have just as easily wound up working for Britain's MI5.

"You know I'm taking an early retirement," he said, breaking the long silence. "End of the year. I've already put a down payment on a small house on the Costa del Sol. I don't think I'm going to miss this much. A few people like yourself maybe, but that's all. I'll give you the address and if you're ever down that way, you can stop by for a visit."

"I'd like that, Steve."

"So would I." He smiled and turned his face back to the window.

Suddenly, a big truck moved out of the traffic, pulling in close to us. It stopped a few feet in front of the Renault, wedging us between two parked cars and blocking off our view of the building. The gold lettering on the side read *Cygne Meubles,* but if it was a furniture van, they'd certainly picked an odd place to park.

I slipped Wilhelmina out, keeping the Luger low and out of sight.

"Nick," Woodriss said quietly. "I'm not armed. I'm sorry, but I didn't think it would be that kind of job."

I cursed him silently, but said nothing. I was too busy watching the rear-view mirror. Three men were approaching us from behind. They were wearing workman's coveralls, but I don't think they'd ever moved any furniture. It's not easy to carry a sofa and a Stoner light machine gun at the same time.

The tight formation fanned out, with one of them hanging back while the other two moved up, one on either side of the car. They stopped when the muzzles of the A1's were level with the open windows.

"What's the meaning of this?" Woodriss demanded. He sounded like a shocked British tourist who'd just found a dead moth floating in his soup.

But our friends weren't buying it. The one covering Steve prodded him with the gun and said, "Out of the car . . . slowly please . . . and keep your hands up where I can see them."

He spoke with a thick Spanish accent, Colombian possibly or Venezuelan. Both he and his two partners were short and muscular, with swarthy complexions and thick black hair. From their high, angular cheekbones and full lips, I guessed that there was more than just a trace of Indian blood in their ancestry. They opened the car doors for us so we could keep our hands at eye level.

When I'd realized that we didn't have the fire-power to take them on, I'd slipped Wilhelmina under the seat. Anyway, one gun would have been useless against three light machine guns at close range. They had the momentary advantage and I wanted to keep it that way. If we played this right, it could possibly lead me straight to the embassy assassin.

"Don't think I won't inform the proper authorities," Woodriss said in a quivering voice. He was still playing the outraged innocent, trying to gain information and keep them off balance at the same time. "If you think you're going to get away with this," he went on, "I have to warn you that . . ." The rest of the sentence was lost as the butt of the Stoner came crashing down on his face.

Woodriss staggered against the side of the trunk, his broken nose pouring out blood. He wobbled a bit, but managed to stay on his feet. Slowly, so that the move wouldn't be misinterpreted, he eased out the handkerchief from his breast pocket and staunched the bleeding.

The gunman who'd clubbed him smiled and the other two smiled back at him. He was fast and he knew it. Much faster than I'd expected.

They herded us to the rear of the truck, where one of them jumped up on the tailgate and unlocked the twin steel doors. He stepped back about ten feet and motioned us up. "Move it," the man behind me ordered, just in case I hadn't gotten the message.

We climbed in with the other two following at a

safe distance. Then they closed and bolted the doors. From the outside it had looked like a normal moving van, but the dim light from the single Coleman lantern showed me they'd made one major interior alteration. Soundproofing. The walls, ceiling, floor, and doors were all covered with a thick layer of sound-absorbing tiles.

We were on one of the busiest streets in Paris, only a few blocks away from the British and American embassies, and yet they could have started firing all three Stoners and no one would have heard a thing. What we'd walked into was nothing less than a killing ground on wheels.

"I see you're admiring the modifications," the one who had entered first said, smiling. "It was my own idea, and I think, you'll have to admit, a fairly ingenious one. We've used it on several occasions with great success."

"I'm sure you have," I said, looking at him more closely. He was slightly taller than his two companions and his features were more refined. But what really set him apart was his speech—clear, unaccented Middle American.

"University of Minnesota," he said as though he had read my thoughts. "My father and brothers went there also; it's a Rodrigo family tradition. But enough talk about myself. Which one of you would like to start explaining why you were watching Mademoiselle Huntington's apartment?"

"That's ridiculous," Woodriss protested. "I wasn't watching anyone's flat, I was merely waiting for a friend—Mr. Carter here. We were about to take off when you blocked in my car."

"How unfortunate," Rodrigo said, grinning. "A very nice story except for one detail. You've been parked across from the apartment since three this morning. *Nobody* waits for a friend that long."

I could see this wasn't getting us anywhere and that the conclusion to our little chat had already been predetermined. Whatever we said, Rodrigo intended to terminate us right here in the middle of Paris. Still, I needed to keep him talking if we were going to have any chance at all of surviving.

"I think I'd better explain our real reason for being here," I said with quiet resignation. "It might help if you took a look at my wallet first."

"All right," Rodrigo said, "but take it out slowly and keep both hands out as you approach me."

I did as he asked. Rodrigo took the wallet from my hand and motioned me back. He studied it for a moment and then tossed it on the floor. "Amalgamated Press and Wire Services," he said slowly. "I fail to see what that has to do with the situation."

"It's very simple," I said. "Both Woodriss and myself are working on an article, an exposé really, detailing what goes on behind the scenes in the modeling business. I'm sure you know what I mean —models being forced to sleep with agency clients, orgies, drugs, all-expense-paid junkets. Not that I think Miss Huntington is involved in anything like that," I added quickly. "It's just that as a fellow American I'd hoped she'd be able to help me make a few contacts. I called her several times, but she refused to meet with me. I thought maybe if we met face to face, seemingly by chance, she might be more willing to talk."

Rodrigo stared at me for a moment and then laughed. "You show more imagination than your friend, Mr. Carter, but your story is still full of holes. Why didn't Woodriss here go after Gail when he saw her leaving this morning? Another man followed her, but he just stayed where he was and continued to watch the house. You see, we also had someone watching Miss Huntington—someone who was already here when your two friends arrived."

"Perhaps you're with a rival news service?" I suggested. I didn't mind playing dumb, just as long as I could keep him talking.

"Hardly, Mr. Carter. I have a great deal of money invested in Gail and like any good business man, I like to keep an eye on my investments. Perhaps now you'd care to have *one* more try at explaining yourself?"

I shook my head. "I told you the truth. If you can't accept it, then there's nothing else to say."

I'd stalled long enough to accomplish what I had in mind. The single Coleman lantern had given me the idea. It really only illuminated a small area of the van and if I could position myself where *part* of my body was in shadow, I'd be able to gradually ease Hugo out of my chamois arm-sheath and into my hand. I could have done it easily by flicking my wrist, but that would have taken a split second, a split second I couldn't spare. I had to have it *in* my hand when we made our move. Otherwise, the Stoners would cut us down where we stood.

I'd managed it with the press card. After I'd handed it to Rodrigo, I'd moved back close to where I'd been standing before. Only now I was about a foot and a half closer to the wall. My right arm and shoulder were just outside the light spill. With my captor paying more attention to Rodrigo than to me, I soon had the pencil-thin stiletto resting comfortably in my hand. Now all I had to do was signal Steve so we could move in unison. But we hadn't worked together in years and I couldn't think of *one* damn code word that would send him into action.

"This is very disappointing," Rodrigo said softly. "I had hoped that one of you would be a little more forthright. Because I *am* going to find out why you've been spying on Gail. After Juan and Fredrico finish with you, you'll be begging to tell me. They always enjoy these things—the simple pleasure of primitive amusements—but believe me, *you* won't enjoy it. Is there anything else you want to say, Carter?"

There was, but not to Rodrigo. I had finally found the right word for Steve: "Harrow."

We both dived at the same time. I came in low, under the muzzle of the Stoner, burying Hugo to the hilt in the Indian's stomach. He screamed and twisted as I raised him over my head, his legs kicking frantically. The A1 slipped from his grasp, letting loose a burst of rapid fire as it clattered to the floor.

I hurled the dying man at Rodrigo, who fired wildly, stitching a bloody line across the flying corpse. The impact of the body knocked him to the floor and sent the Stoner skating across the tiles. At least for the moment, Rodrigo was out of the game.

I turned just in time to see the other Indian snap Woodriss's neck. It made a sharp cracking sound and then his watery blue eyes went dead. The Indian let him fall to the floor and turned to face me.

We were both about six feet from where one of the Stoners lay between us. I began to move slowly forward with Hugo in my hand, the long, thin blade smeared with blood. The Indian grinned, reached behind his back, and came out with his fist wrapped around a wicked-looking ebony-handled dagger.

He went into a crouch as we closed in on the machine gun, his knife hand feinting and jabbing. I knew what he was trying to do—he was trying to keep me from looking at Rodrigo. There'd been just enough time for him to recover and shove the body off. Maybe he was already bringing the Stoner into firing position.

I raised Hugo and threw it in a spinning arch that drove it into the Indian's chest just below the breastbone. He let out a shrill, piercing scream as a crimson stain began to spread across the front of his coveralls. He tried to pull the stiletto out, but his legs buckled and he hit the floor with an echoing crash.

I dove, rolled, and came up with the Stoner in

my hand. I swung it toward the rear of the van where I knew Rodrigo would be waiting for me. But it turned out I was wrong. He wasn't waiting to blow me away and he wasn't still pinned beneath the dead Indian—in fact, he wasn't there at all.

I held on to the Stoner and probed the shadows, walking a complete circuit of the van. There was no place for him to hide; just a few packing cases scattered about, none of them large enough to conceal a man. Then I saw it—a thin strip of light about three feet long where the floor and wall came together.

I moved in from the side and cautiously pushed the wall above the line. It gave way under my hand and daylight flooded the interior of the truck. A built-in escape hatch. Rodrigo had decided not to hang around and see how the fighting came out. He'd done a "rabbit" on his friends, turning tail and scurrying to safety even though the odds were on their side.

Turning away from the escape hatch, I walked over to where Steve lay sprawled out on his side. I rolled him onto his back and closed his bloodshot eyes. Then, almost without thinking, I reached down and straightened the school tie he'd always been so proud of. During the last few years, he hadn't been much more than a burn-out shell of a man who drank to keep his ghosts at bay. Still, he hadn't lost his nerve or tried to make a run for it. Despite everything that had happened to him, he would never be one of the Rodrigos of this world.

I left Woodriss and pulled Hugo out of the

Indian's chest, wiping the blade clean on his coveralls before I slipped it back into my arm-sheath. It was time to get out of this charnal house on wheels. I retrieved my wallet and pushed open the escape hatch, jumping down into the sun-filled street.

I walked back to the Renault for Wilhelmina and then made a phone call in a nearby café. In about ten minutes, two men in work clothes would come and drive the "furniture" van away. Steve would get a decent, if somewhat quiet burial, and maybe the AXE lab crew would come up with a lead or two from their examination of the truck.

"Harrow," I said under my breath as I crossed the cobblestoned-courtyard of number 20 Avenue Gabriel. I'd known Steve would move on that word because it meant so much to him. Harrow . . . the name of the English school he'd attended.

Chapter Eight

I stood outside Gail Huntington's door and listened to the sound of the bell fade back into silence. That was the third time I'd rung it. Either she wasn't back yet or she wasn't opening the door to unexpected callers. It didn't make any difference to me. I knelt down and picked the "burglar-proof" double-lock system in just under two minutes.

The door swung open on well-oiled hinges, revealing a circular foyer with a polished marble floor and twin Empire side-tables, each one bearing a large vase of freshly cut flowers.

"Miss Huntington," I called out, moving through the archway and into the living room. It also was deserted, but the furnishings told me something about the owner. There were pillows everywhere, large and small ones in different shades of pastel silk. They were piled up in corners and scattered over the couch along with almost a dozen fur and sheepskin rugs. She was obviously the kind of woman who liked things soft, comfortable, and not too far out of reach.

Then there were the ashtrays. Every one I saw was filled to overflowing with crushed-out butts, each of the filters ringed with deep-red lipstick smears. Maybe she was a lousy housekeeper or just damn nervous. Considering the way Hector had treated her last night, nervous seemed the most likely choice.

There was nothing unusual about the guest room, kitchen, or bath, but the master bedroom had several interesting touches. Like a fully stocked wet bar in one corner and the huge mirror suspended over the king-sized bed. She hadn't had a chance to make it before she left. The pale-blue satin sheets were rumpled and twisted as if she'd spent a restless night. Next to it on the floor, an empty Moët bottle floated on the surface of a water-filled ice bucket.

I had a feeling that she spent most of her time here and it seemed as good a place as any to start a thorough search. Ten minutes later I knew I'd been right when I found the false-bottomed antique dresser. It took me a while to figure out how to open it, but finally I twisted one of the rosette-carved knobs and a deep wooden tray slid out.

There was nothing feminine or soft about its contents: a Russian Dragunov, one of the few semi-automatic rifles specifically designed for sniping; and three handguns—a Luger, a snub-nosed Colt, and a single-action Smith and Wesson .357. All four of them were perfect weapons for killing at a certain range. I checked over each of them carefully; they were all loaded, spotlessly clean, and in perfect working order. There were also four full boxes of ammo stacked in the drawer beside them.

The innocent explanation, the one her data sheet provided, was that she was just a "gun nut" who liked to test her marksmanship in competitive shooting events. But her little arsenal was also something else—it was every type of weapon a professional assassin would ever need.

I put everything back the way I'd found it and slid the drawer back into place. It took me an hour to search the rest of the apartment, but I didn't turn up anything worth a second glance. It was almost noon, time for me to collect the Ferrari and drive over to the other stakeout.

I locked up, using the picks again, and had just slipped them back in my pocket when I heard the sound of the elevator doors sliding open.

I quickly put my finger to the bell as a cool, feminine voice asked, "What the hell do you think you're doing?"

Chapter Nine

I turned around and smiled. "Miss Huntington?" I asked tenatively.

"Yes, I'm Gail Huntington. Now would you mind telling me what you're doing here? The concierge has instructions not to let anyone past the desk without phoning me first. And *never*," she added tersely, "to allow anyone up here if I'm not home."

"I didn't see any concierge," I said, shrugging. That was true enough; I'd picked the lock on the service door and come up the back stairs. "I would have waited in the lobby," I went on, "but since we had an appointment, I figured you were expecting me."

"Appointment?" She repeated the word with a puzzled expression on her face.

"Yes," I said, smiling again. "Don't you remember? I'm Nick Carter, Amalgamated Press and Wire Services." I flipped open my wallet and held it out so she could see the ID card.

"I still don't understand," she said slowly, but

there was no hostility in her voice now.

Seeing her close-up for the first time, I couldn't help wondering how anyone that beautiful could have anything in common with Rodrigo and Hector. But then, money and politics make for some pretty strange relationships. On this morning she was dressed in beige slacks and a rust-colored silk blouse that complimented her shining chestnut-brown hair. She wore surprisingly little makeup for a model, and the only jewelry she had on was a simple gold chain around her neck. I guess when you look *that* good, you don't need a lot of extras.

"I called you last month," I continued, "and we set up an interview for noon today. It's for the article I'm doing on successful American women working in Paris. Does that sound familiar?"

"Frankly, no. Not that I doubt your word," she added quickly. "It's just that I've been very busy lately and sometimes these things slip my mind. If it won't take too long, I'll be happy to talk with you."

"Half an hour at most."

She fished a ring of keys out of her shoulder bag and unlocked the door. "After you," she said, stepping to the side. She'd moved just enough to let me by, but not without brushing up against her. If that was the way she wanted to play it, it was fine with me. I slid past, my leg grazing her thigh. She'd done it casually, but it was one of the most sexual split seconds I'd ever spent with my clothes on.

"We can talk in the living room," she said, leading me across the foyer with her hand on my arm.

"I usually have a glass of wine around this time of day. Would you care to join me?"

"Thanks, but don't go any trouble on my account."

"It's no bother," she said, flashing me a warm smile. "Just make yourself comfortable and I'll be right back."

I watched her make a graceful exit, her hips swaying gently as she strode through the arched door that led to the kitchen. Pushing some of the pillows aside, I settled down on the couch and lit a cigarette. I needed a minute or two to think this thing through.

She'd fallen for my "appointment" story, or at least it seemed that way on the surface. But there were a few other factors to be considered. Like the strong possibility that she was the graveyard sniper who'd blown Julot away and that she recognized me as the man who'd come to meet him. Or that she'd been in contact with Rodrigo and had *let* me talk my way in.

The transition from hostile to more than friendly had been a little too sudden for my taste. Maybe the smiles, the wine, and the come-on were all a part of her act. If so, she was damn good at it. I'd been in this type of situation many times before. About one out of every six had turned out to be a setup—an attempt to get classified information, or else to terminate me. I'd probably know within the next hour: business as usual or just another victim of Carter's boyish charm?

I heard the tap of her heels returning from the

kitchen. I quickly unstrapped Wilhelmina and Hugo and slipped them under a pillow. If she was going to try some more body language on me, I didn't want to have to take time out for awkward explanations. But if things turned sour, the Luger and stiletto were still close at hand.

"Now that didn't take so long," she said, re-entering the room. She was carrying an open red bottle of *Pouilly-Fuissé* in one hand and a pair of long-stemmed glasses in the other. "Will you pour, Nick?" she asked, offering me the bottle.

"My pleasure." I filled both glasses to the halfway point, leaving room enough to savor the bouquet. There was another, stronger scent nearby. Gail had daubed on perfume, a heady, exotic fragrance that reminded me of the jungle. She also had decided we were now on a first-name basis.

"You don't have to rush with the interview," she said softly. "I phoned the agency and told them to cancel my afternoon shooting. I thought it was the least I could do under the circumstances. I'm usually not that rude, or forgetful. Honest."

"You don't have to apologize," I told her. "It's just as much my fault. I should have called you yesterday and confirmed it. I really appreciate your giving me the extra time."

"I wouldn't have it any other way," she said in a breathy whisper.

The message was clear enough. If I wanted her, I could have her. And I did want her, even if the phone call she'd just told me about was to Rodrigo and not to the Agency Castel.

She picked up her wine and sat down beside me. At close range her perfume was almost overpowering. Images flashed through my mind— a dark, sweltering rain forest; a jaguar stalking its prey; a rough stone altar. All of them seemed appropriate for Gail Huntington.

"Well," she said pleasantly, "what would you like to know? I've done a number of interviews before, but everyone seems to have a different set of questions. Some of which I wouldn't answer, even for you."

"Don't worry," I said, laughing. "I'm doing this for a family-oriented magazine. Since we have plenty of time, why don't we start at the beginning? The agency told me something about your background. . . that you were what we used to call an 'army brat' and that as a teenager you were a prize-winning handgun and rifle shot."

"That's right. My father was an Army weaponry instructor. While the other girls on the base were still playing with dolls, he had me out on the range blasting away at targets with his .45 service revolver. Since he couldn't have a son," she said, grinning, "he had to settle for a tomboy."

"He must be very proud of you."

"If he were still alive he would be," she said in a cold, flat voice. "He died five years ago. He was on his way home one night when three *black bastards* jumped him in the base parking lot. They razored him so bad that he bled to death before they could get him to a hospital."

The bitterness and hatred there was so intense I

could almost feel it. Her eyes burned with rage undiminished by time.

"Did the MP's catch them?" I asked softly.

"Yes, and it's lucky they did because *I* was out looking for the sons of bitches myself. But the MP's got to them first. They had a trial, even though that kind doesn't deserve it. All three of them pulled ten years hard time with a dishonorable discharge at the end of it. But that wasn't nearly enough as far as I was concerned. They should have shot them, right?"

Instead of answering the question, I quickly asked another. "Was it a random act of violence or did some kind of motive come out at the trial?"

"Motive, shit," she said harshly. "They were three recruits, just backwoods trash. My dad had been having a little fun with them during gunnery practice that morning. I guess a few of the boys got carried away, roughed them up a little. But hell, it wasn't anything to get crazy over."

There wasn't much I could say. I'd been in the Deep South too many times to accept her story at face value. In spite of all the new laws and reforms, there were still a few twisted types left who liked their "fun", most of it failing under the categories of arson, assault, and rape. The real shame of it was that the South had changed. There were just some people too afraid to change with it.

"Pour me some more wine," she said, holding out her glass. "Every time I start talking about my father's death I feel like bustin' loose, squeezing the trigger on an M-16 and not easin' up until the magazine is empty. I guess we'd better not talk about it anymore," she added in a softer voice. "And I don't have to tell you that everything I just said is strictly off-the-record."

"Don't worry," I assured her. "I wouldn't even consider writing about something as personal as that. What I'm after is a profile, not an exposé." I refilled both our glasses, emptying the bottle. "Tell me," I said casually, "do you get to do much competition shooting over here?"

"None at all," she answered quickly. "I don't really have the time anymore. In fact, I sold my gun collection before I moved to Paris. I can't even remember the last time I held a gun, let alone fired one."

"Too bad," I said, trying to sound disappointed. "It would have made an interesting angle for the story."

One thing about Gail—she lied well. If I hadn't uncovered her personal arsenal, I would have sworn she was telling the truth. That didn't make me feel very comfortable about the phone call she'd made from the kitchen.

"Losing interest?" she asked. I think she meant it to be seductive, but there was a petulant undertone to the question.

"No," I said, grinning. "I was just lost in thought for a moment."

"Thinking about me?"

"No one else," I answered truthfully.

"You know you could have been a model yourself, Nick. Not the pretty-boy type—your face has

too much character for that. No," she said softly,
"it would have to be something rough and masculine."

She put down her wine glass and began to slowly
run her fingertips over the contours of my face.
"Rough and masculine," she whispered again,
"that's what attracts me."

I slipped my arm around her and pulled her
close. Our lips met, gently at first, but then we
began kissing with a kind of wild hunger. Her
mouth was dry and hot, her tongue eager and prob-
ing. She squirmed in my grasp, brushing against
me in a slow, sensuous rhythm.

Pushing me away, she suddenly stood up on the
couch. She teetered a little on her high heels until
she balanced herself with a hand against the wall.
"Watch," she said in a throaty whisper.

Her nimble fingers quickly undid the buttons on
her blouse. She pushed it back off her shoulders,
letting it fall on the floor. Wiggling her hips, she
slipped out of her slacks in even less time. She
wasn't wearing anything underneath. Her long,
supple body was evenly tanned to a deep golden
brown.

The discarded blouse also had concealed a broad
silver armband that encircled her arm just above
the elbow. It was crude beaten-silver, probably
hammered out by some local Indian craftsman in
the Andes. A single rough-edged piece of jade had
been mounted in the center.

"That never comes off," she said with a mocking
grin. Standing over me with her hands on her hips,

she looked like an Amazon, or some savage and defiant goddess about to accept a sacrifice from her followers.

I undressed, palming the tiny gas bomb attached to my thigh as I slipped out of my trousers. I tucked it behind a cushion, reached out, and pulled Gail down onto the couch.

There was nothing gentle about our love-making. We came together, our bodies coupling in furious, unthinking abandon. Gail twisted and moaned, her arms locked around me and her long nails digging into my back. The rhythm built quickly to a pounding, savage tempo. She looked up at me with her mouth in a half-open smile, her deep green eyes bright with pleasure.

We slipped off the couch and onto the floor. Both of us were glistening with sweat now and holding on to each other all the more tightly.

In the frenzy of climax we knocked over the empty wine bottle. It hit the table edge with a loud, sharp crack and shattered over the rug. Neither Gail or I even bothered to look in that direction. We were still together, motionless now; the room strangely silent except for the short, shallow sounds of our breathing.

When we drew apart, she padded into the bedroom and came back with a thick white bath towel. "Dry yourself off," she said, tossing it to me. "I'll be back in a few minutes."

I nodded and returned her smile. I had a feeling she was headed for the shower and I was starting to wonder why I hadn't been invited along. We'd already ruled out modesty, so maybe it was just something she preferred doing on a solo basis.

Another possibility was that the time had come for something unpleasant to happen. Now was certainly the ideal moment for it. My weapons were all tucked away under the pillows and I was naked, something that always gives the clothed assailant a psychological advantage.

I retrieved the Luger and briskly rubbed myself dry, knotting the towel around my waist when I finished. Traffic noises floated up from the avenue, while down the hallway I heard the sound of a shower being turned on full blast.

I dressed quickly, putting all three of my weapons back in their proper places. I was still half expecting Rodrigo or Gail herself to make a sudden reappearance. Not carrying wine this time, but her nasty little snub-nosed Colt. Maybe it sounds paranoid, but unless you're prepared for *all* the possibilities your chances of surviving in this business are pretty bleak.

"You were good," she said, emerging from the hallway some ten minutes later. "I might even say excellent, but I'd have to get to know you better first."

I suppose she meant it as a compliment. Only her tone of voice made it sound as though she were passing judgment on the Pouilly-Fuissé we'd had earlier. At least I had gotten a better-than-average rating.

"So were you," I said quietly. I knew she'd expected me to say something in return and besides, if you like them wild, it was an accurate enough appraisal.

Gail tossed back her head and laughed. "I already know that, Nick. Still, it's nice of you to say so."

"My pleasure. Don't let it go to your head, though."

We both laughed and Gail crossed the room to sit next to me on the couch. Her shower had washed away the jungle scent, leaving her smelling as fresh and clean as a schoolgirl. She'd put on a white-silk wraparound robe and had pinned up her hair at the back. The savage goddess was once again a sophisticated Parisian woman.

"I guess the modeling business has given me more than my share of ego," she admitted with a rueful smile. "It's hard to keep it under control. People are always telling you you're gorgeous . . . beautiful . . . perfect. After awhile it becomes almost impossible to accept anything less."

"I understand," I said, holding out my cigarette case. "In fact, it's a good angle for my story, if you don't mind my using it?"

"No, that's fine. As long as you don't make me look like too much of an egomaniac," she added quickly.

"Don't worry, I promise I won't."

She took one of my cigarettes, her hand trembling as she fumbled with the metal clip that holds them in the case. She could barely keep it steady when I lit it for her—the end dipped and danced in and out of the flame.

After the way we'd spent the last hour, I would have expected her to be more relaxed than anything else. Now, suddenly, Gail Huntington had a very bad case of the shakes.

"You'd better go now," she said quietly. "If you call me later in the week we can set up a time for finishing the interview."

"Whatever you say." I could feel the room temperature rapidly dropping to below freezing. This was certainly a very changeable lady. I leaned over and kissed her chastely on the forehead. In return she gave me a weak, half-hearted smile.

"Talk to you soon," I said, rising to my feet.

"So long." The two words came out in a barely audible whisper.

I had my hand on the doorknob when I heard her call out my name.

I quickly retraced my steps. She was sitting where I'd left her just a moment ago, only now she had her arms wrapped around herself as if she were shivering from the cold.

"Is there something wrong, Gail?"

She stared at me; from the look in her eyes I knew she was making some kind of decision. "No," she said finally, "there's nothing wrong. I thought you'd forgotten your cigarette case . . . that's all. You'd better get out of here now, please."

It was a feeble, transparent lie. Nothing at all like her earlier performance.

On the way downstairs I couldn't help thinking

about how she had called my name. I'd never heard it spoken quite that way before. With desperation and fear is the best way I can describe it.

Chapter Ten

I spent the rest of the afternoon with the stakeout team covering Hector. Before I arrived only two things had happened worth noting: one dull, the other very interesting.

"He went out to lunch," Bellows informed me in his usual laconic manner. "Came out of the building at exactly one and walked directly to a restaurant four blocks away on Rue Valadon. That was the first time any of us had seen him since we took up our positions last night."

"Did anything happen at the restaurant?" I prompted. Getting information out of Jeff Bellows took patience—lots of patience. Still, I had asked to have him assigned to the stakeout because he was the most accurate and painstaking surveillance man we had in the Paris area.

"He ate," Bellows said finally. "Snails, a casserole, and half a carafe of Tavel to wash it down. O'Neil got a seat at the bar and kept him under observation the whole time. The only time Hector spoke was when he ordered his meal from the *patron*. When he finished he walked straight back to his apartment."

"I hope that's not the *interesting* item," I said with a rueful smile. "I'd really hate to hear the dull one."

Bellows shook his head and took another minute to relight his pipe with that "flame-thrower" lighter of his that had already charred away half the bowl. There was no point in prodding him. It only made for a longer wait in the end.

"He had a visitor," Bellows continued when the pipe was finally drawing right. "A male in his mid- to late-thirties, five-ten, stocky, with bone structure, skin, and hair color suggesting mestizo ancestry. He was wearing a tan raincoat over workman's coveralls. Also, he walked as though he were experiencing pain or discomfort. If I were to hazard a guess, which I rarely do, I'd say he'd been in a fight recently."

"I can put a name to your man," I told him. "Rodrigo. He and a couple of his hoods killed Steve Woodriss about three hours ago."

After a moment's silence Bellows said, "I'll keep that in mind." He and Woodriss had been friends. The way he spoke the simple phrase made it sound like a death sentence.

"This is a hands-off operation," I reminded him. "At least for the time being."

Bellows nodded and went on with his report. "Rodrigo arrived at two-fourteen and rang Hector's apartment from the lobby. Hector came down to meet him and the pair walked around the gardens of the Champ de Mars for about twenty minutes. I couldn't risk getting anyone in close enough to eavesdrop," he added apologetically, "but from the way they were gesturing I'd say both men were highly agitated. When they split up, I put O'Neil on Rodrigo and followed Hector back to the apartment myself."

"Does their garden stroll suggest anything to you?" I asked.

"We're obviously thinking along the same lines," Bellows replied with a wan smile. "They're more afraid that Hector's apartment is bugged than they are of being seen together. Otherwise, why talk in a public place when you can do it in private?"

"Exactly. Here's what I want you to do, Jeff. The next time our friend goes out, check the place for bugs. If an electronic sweep doesn't turn any up, then plant one of our *own*. If you do find some, then leave them and try to locate the listening post. Clear enough?"

"I'll handle it personally."

I sat with Bellows in the tiny Austin for two more hours. Apart from acquiring a strong aversion to the maple-scented pipe tobacco he smoked, I got nothing for my troubles. Finally I gave up, collected the Ferrari, and headed back to the hotel.

The streets were clogged with commuter traffic. I ignored the blaring horns and curses that were standard fare in the Paris rush hour, concentrating instead on what had happened that day. Despite the noise, the city had a calming effect on me. Overhead, the low skyline glowed with sunset color that was broken only by the Eiffel Tower and the white-stone basilica of the Sacré Coeur.

One thing I knew for certain now—that Gail Huntington, Hector, and Rodrigo were all connected in some way. Linking together what I'd witnessed last night at the Agency Castel, the "death truck" incident, and my encounter with Gail, the whole thing added up to a conspiracy. But a conspiracy to what end? There were still too many factors that didn't set right. The embassy assassinations were the work of top-flight professionals. Would they use someone like Gail with her volatile, unstable nature and frequent mood-swings?

In spite of the way he had set up the truck, Rodrigo, too, was an amateur. A real pro would have searched me and found Hugo strapped to my arm. Hector was a hard case, an enforcer with more muscle than brains. So if they *were* the group that had been terminating Third World diplomats so successfully, then who was the master planner, the puppeteer concealed in the shadows who pulled all the strings?

It was a question I would have to answer soon. The Arab oil summit was only two days away.

I garaged the Ferrari and went up to my room. Wes Dryer was sitting on a window ledge at the end of the corridor. He smiled, waved, and came forward to meet me.

"Anything happening?" I asked.

Lauren's shadow for the day shook his head. "She only left the room once to pick up some cigarettes and a paper at the counter in the lobby."

"Okay. Thanks, Wes, I'll take over now. You're back on duty at the same time tomorrow."

As I turned to unlock the door, the lanky field agent put a restraining hand on my arm. "Nick," he said, grinning, "is this really a top security tail-job or just some pretty lady you're worried about?"

"A little of both," I admitted, smiling. "But that doesn't mean you shouldn't take it seriously. She's been through a lot and I'm still not sure there isn't more to come. I wouldn't have asked you to be here if I didn't think she needed round-the-clock protection."

"I wasn't questioning your judgment," he said defensively. "If you say she needs watching, that's good enough for me." Before I could say anything else, he turned on his heel and hurried down the stairs.

I found the object of our conversation sitting out on the balcony. She was dressed in her suede jeans, accompanied by one of my shirts with the sleeves rolled up. When she heard my footsteps behind her, she jumped up and ran into my arms.

"Nick," she said breathlessly, "I've been so worried. I expected you back hours ago. When you didn't phone or anything, I was sure . . . well, I thought something had happened to you."

I held her close and kissed her. Lauren's reprimand made me feel strangely domestic, like some overworked husband who'd stayed too late at the office, totally forgetting that it was *their* night to go out to dinner. It was a pleasant feeling, but one I could never really experience unless I retired from AXE.

Of course, I'd have to find the right woman, too. Lauren? I already knew that I was more involved with her than I ever wanted to admit to myself. Was there any truth in what Wes Dryer had hinted at? Was my desire to protect her professional or personal?

"I'm sorry I'm late," I said truthfully. "I'm going to make it up by taking you to a very posh diplomatic reception. I'll even spring for an evening gown, though I'll have a hell of a time explaining that to the old guy who vests my expense account."

"You're forgiven," she said, kissing me again. "But we'd better get moving—the shops are only open another two hours."

Chapter Eleven

Somalia is one of Africa's newest countries and also one of its poorest. So I wasn't surprised when their consulate turned out to be a modest three-story brick building on Rue Lecourbe.

Even the Rollses and Mercedes lining the curb looked a bit out of place this far over on the Left Bank. But it was definitely where the reception was being held. The sounds of polite conversation and clinking glasses drifted from the open windows on the second floor. And over the main entrance the country's blue and white flag rippled and swayed in the breeze.

"That man's staring at me," Lauren complained in a low whisper. But I could tell from the smile on her face that she was enjoying the attention. In her low-cut evening gown she was worth staring at. It was a deep red silk that left her back and shoulders bare while the soft, flowing fabric emphasized the graceful contours of her body.

"Want me to have a word with him?" I asked. It really wasn't a serious question.

"No," she said quickly. I looked back at the chauffeur who'd been eying her. He grinned and tipped his cap. Paris.

"Your invitation, sir," requested the tall black man guarding the door. I handed it over, noticing when he reached out to take it that he was wearing a gun and shoulder holster under his suit coat. With four diplomats dead already, he probably wasn't the only member of the staff carrying a concealed weapon.

"Just take the elevator to your right," he said, stepping aside to let us pass. "The reception is on the second floor."

Upstairs, the doors opened onto a noisy, crowded room. Among the babble of voices I recognized at least half a dozen languages that I was fairly fluent in. Most of the men and women were in formal attire, but there were also guests dressed in *galabeyas* and brightly colored African *dashikis*. A few heads turned as we entered the room, then quickly looked away again when they realized we weren't important.

The room itself was a curious blend of Eastern and Western cultures. The crystal chandelier, heavy drapes, and furniture were typical of diplomatic decor, but the wall decorations were strictly Somalian. There were carved native staffs and spears, bright squares of hand-woven fabric, and one entire wall lined with long wooden prayer boards.

"Look," Lauren said, tugging at my sleeve. "There're Ann-Marie and Christine. And I think they're heading our way." I turned in the direction Lauren indicated and got my first look at the two women. It was difficult to say who was the more beautiful.

Christine Dalton was a statuesque blonde with icy pale-blue eyes. Dark and intense were the best ways I could describe Ann-Marie Michaels. Her hair was thick and black, cascading down to her shoulders in curls. Neither one of their photographs did them justice.

"Who's their escort?"

"I don't know," Lauren whispered. Both models were with a tall, white-haired man who was wearing a tuxedo. As the trio drew nearer they all smiled.

"Lauren, what a surprise to see you," Christine Dalton said in French. "I didn't realize you moved in these lofty circles."

"Then you must have a very limited social life," Lauren retorted. She wasn't about to let the blonde model get away with anything.

"Nice to see you, Lauren," Ann-Marie said, deftly slipping in-between the two combatants. "Don't mind Christine. She saw a wrinkle this morning and it's soured her entire day."

Lauren and Ann-Marie laughed while Christine silently glared at them. To help ease the tension, I stopped a passing waiter with a tray-load of champagne and handed out glasses to everyone.

Christine tossed hers back in one gulp and grabbed another one from the retreating waiter. "What a lovely gown," she said, looking Lauren over from head to toe. "Something like that must have cost an entire month's wages. It must be difficult to save that much on an office girl's salary. Or did your *patron* buy it for you? For services rendered," she added softly.

I knew it was going to happen. With a flick of her wrist, Lauren threw her champagne in Christine's face. A moment of stunned silence followed.

"Bitch," Christine said through clenched teeth, "you'd better start looking for a new job tomorrow. Because I'm going to make sure you're fired from the agency."

"I quit yesterday," Lauren said, smiling. That wasn't really true, but I knew she didn't want to give Christine the satisfaction of having her dismissed.

The tall blonde accepted a handkerchief from her escort and began to dry her face. The champagne had caused little damage; her make-up was streaked in a few places and there were a couple of spots on her turquoise silk dress. Still, she was staring at Lauren as if she would like to murder her.

Ann-Marie Michaels noticed it too. "Why don't we get another drink," she suggested, slipping her arm through Lauren's. "It's cooler out on the balcony and we can talk there. That is," she added, smiling at me, "if your handsome escort doesn't mind?"

"Nick?"

"Go ahead," I said in English. "I'll come out and join you in a while."

As the two women began to tread their way through the crowd, the white-haired man said, "Please excuse my manners. I don't believe we've been introduced. Colonel Victor Épernay."

"Nick Carter." I grasped the gloved hand he extended and found it stiff and unyielding. An artificial replacement, plastic or possibly wood.

"A souvenir of Dien Bien Phu," he explained with a tight smile. "Monsieur Carter, Mademoiselle Dalton." The cool blonde acknowledged the introduction with a brief nod.

"Were you also in Indochina, Monsieur Carter? Or as you Americans now call it, Vietnam? I only ask," he added, "because you have that hard, competent look about you. The look of a veteran."

"I spent some time in Southeast Asia," I answered evasively. I had come to the reception for a look at Christine and Ann-Marie. What I'd seen so far was interesting, but I didn't want to get sidetracked listening to war stories or a lecture on France's former colonial glory.

"Perhaps Monsieur Carter would find the conversation more stimulating if he'd lost a brother in the war as I did?" Christine said softly.

"That was twenty-seven years ago," Épernay quietly reminded her. "I remember because I was there, but you weren't even born then, child."

"Don't talk down to me," Christine said angrily. Before the Colonel could defend himself, she turned away and was lost in the crowd.

"Deserted on all sides," Épernay said with a

weary smile. "Christine was always a sensitive child, and a spoiled child in many ways. Her parents died in an automobile accident less than a year after she was born. Christine was raised by a maiden aunt who gave her all the comforts, luxuries even, but not much in the way of real affection."

"Then she feels her brother was part of a family she never had?"

The Colonel nodded. "He served under me in Indochina. Not a bad soldier, but not a great one either. In her mind, Christine has turned him into this noble and heroic figure. Actually, that's how we came to know each other. She found out I was her brother's commanding officer and came by to visit, wanting to know what I could tell her about him. Perhaps because of her beauty, I told her pretty much what she wanted to hear."

"I don't blame you," I said, grinning, "but I'm surprised to find her here. Her brother died defending the colonial way of life. Somalia was a former colony of both the British and the Italians. If she feels that strongly about it, she can hardly have much love for Somalia or any other emerging nation."

Épernay shrugged. "Women. I'm almost seventy and I still don't understand them. I know that doesn't answer your question, Monsieur Carter, but it's the best I can do. Perhaps she comes to keep an old man company. At least I'd like to think so."

I decided it was time to change the subject.

"What about Ann-Marie?" I asked. "Don't tell me you're cornering the market on beautiful fashion models."

"No," he said, laughing. "Ann-Marie came with her young man who works in the Ministry of Defense. I know her well through Christine, though. A charming girl, very considerate and generous. As much a peacemaker as Christine is a trouble-maker."

"No colonial hang-ups?"

"I doubt if she even knows enough to find Somalia on the map. Ann-Marie is more interested in a good time than in politics. Sometimes," he added wistfully, "I wish Christine had the same good sense."

I was about to ask him another question when I caught sight of a familiar figure on the other side of the room. I excused myself and began to work my way through the crowd. The party was in full swing now and I lost track of my objective twice before I finally managed to catch up with her.

"Gail," I said, tapping her on the shoulder.

She whirled around, the welcoming smile on her face tightening into a hard line as she recognized me. "Well, if it isn't Mr. Carter, the *reporter*. What are you doing now," she asked, "trying to round out your story by barging in on my social life?"

I shook my head. "I just came over to say hello. You seemed upset when I left this afternoon, so I wanted to make sure you were all right."

"How considerate," she said with a mocking smile. "But you really needn't have bothered. I have Rodrigo here to take care of all my problems. I believe you two have already met?"

I'd been aware of someone standing behind me ever since I approached Gail. I turned around and saw the stocky mestizo, who'd exchanged his coveralls for a tuxedo and ruffled shirt. His right hand was thrust deep in his pocket, wrapped around some object. Possibly a gun.

"How's the trucking business?" I asked him.

He glared at me, then forced himself to smile. "Ah, the famous American humor. I hope your friend, the Englishman, enjoyed our meeting this afternoon."

"He's dead," I said quietly. "I'm surprised that you don't remember. Of course, you were in such a hurry to leave that it probably all seems pretty vague to you. If you're still wondering what happened to the guy you left behind," I added, "you can stop wondering now."

"A momentary advantage, Carter. Why don't you make the best use of it and leave Paris tonight."

I was suddenly getting very tired of this amateur tough act. I reached out and grabbed his arm just above the elbow, my fingers locking in on the pressure points.

Rodrigo began to squirm, trying to break my grip with his free hand. I twisted him around and pushed the other arm behind his back. His face began to turn red and he sucked in air in noisy gulps. In a second or two he would begin to scream from the pain.

I eased up on the pressure points and yanked his right hand out of his pocket. A Smith and Wesson Airweight came tumbling out after it. I caught it before it could hit the floor and tucked away the "purse gun" in my dinner-jacket pocket.

"Did you have to do that?" Gail asked angrily.

"You want some advice? Find somebody else to take care of your problems."

I turned back to Rodrigo, who was gently massaging his arm. "A momentary advantage," he repeated. "Things will be different when next we meet."

"Rodrigo," I said, smiling, "you've been watching too many American gangster movies."

After meeting the Avenue Gabriel gang again, the air out on the balcony seemed particularly fresh and clean. I found Lauren talking to a tall, imposing black man. Ann-Marie Michaels was nowhere in sight.

"There you are," she said, waving me over. "Nick, this is Ali Agabar, the consul general. He's just been telling me something about his country."

"Boring you is more like it," he said with a deep rumbling laugh. He was about a half-inch taller than I, with broad shoulders and a pot belly that strained the buttons on his tuxedo jacket. His round ebony face was intelligent and friendly; his clipped British accent the only reminder of his former rulers.

"But I wasn't bored," Lauren protested.

"Perhaps not," said Agabar. "But I have to watch myself constantly. I find it easy to get carried away extolling Somalia's numerous virtues. Nice meeting you, Mr. Carter. Now if you'll excuse me, I must circulate among my other guests."

"What a charming man," Lauren said as we watched him walk away.

"I'm glad you've been enjoying yourself. What happened to Ann-Marie?"

Lauren shrugged. "She probably went to look for her boyfriend. She was here when I started talking to Monsieur Agabar, but when I turned around to say something to her she was gone. Will you answer a question for me, Nick?"

"If I can."

"Did you know Ann-Marie and Christine were going to be here? And Gail, too; I saw you talking to her before you came out here."

"I assumed that they would be," I answered truthfully. Unless I was mistaken, there was an edge of jealousy in Lauren's voice.

"Then this really isn't our evening," she continued. "You're here because *they're* here."

"I could have come by myself," I said, slipping my arm around her waist. "But I thought you'd enjoy this."

"I am, Nick. But the point is—"

Whatever it was, she never got to finish it. Suddenly the lights went out, in a split second the crowded room was in total darkness, as if someone had slammed down the lid on a coffin.

"Stay here," I said, grabbing Lauren's arm. "This is the safest place for you until the lights come back on."

I took out my Luger and began to move cautiously forward. People were already beginning to spill out onto the balcony. The crowd inside was restless, milling aimlessly about. I heard giggles, apologies, and curses in a dozen or more tongues. So far, no one had panicked. I wondered if they realized this was no ordinary blackout.

I cleared the French doors and started to work my way toward the center of the room. My progress was even slower now that I was inside. I tucked Wilhelmina in my belt so I could have both hands free; a few seconds later, I used them to catch a woman who'd tripped and nearly sent us both sprawling to the floor.

"Your attention please!" The deep booming voice was Agabar's. As far as I could tell, he was on the opposite side of the room from me, about fifteen feet away. The crowd quieted down quickly, everyone standing still.

"First," he continued, "please accept my apologies for this momentary inconvenience. My staff assures me that it is merely a burnt-out fuse and that the lights will be back on in another minute or so. As soon as they are the party will go on as before. Please stay and enjoy yourselves. Thank you."

Several people applauded the brief speech and there seemed to be a collective sigh, an easing of tension in the room. Many of those present had been at the scene of one or more of the diplomatic murders. Any unexpected occurrence, especially a blackout, was bound to make them edgy.

It was beginning to look like I was wrong. I'd immediately assumed that the power failure was part of a plan, a deep cover for yet another assassination. But so far there were no signs that anything like that had happened.

Overhead, the chandelier lights flickered once, twice, and then came back on for good. The crowd let out a ragged cheer and started moving again, mostly toward the bar. Everyone began talking, but then suddenly stopped as a loud, piercing scream cut through the din like a knife blade.

I turned toward its source. An elderly woman was sobbing on some man's shoulder, and just beyond her three men were bending over something on the floor. I pushed my way through the crowd and finally saw what it was.

Even in death, Ali Agabar looked imposing. His face was solemn, almost stern as it stared up at the ceiling. His two big hands were clutched around the triangular wooden handle of an icepick. I couldn't see the blade at all. It was buried to the hilt in his chest, where it had undoubtedly punctured his heart on contact.

"Mon Dieu," Lauren whispered, suddenly appearing at my side.

"I don't think God had anything to do with it," I told her. "We'd better get out of here before the gendarmes arrive."

Chapter Twelve

When I collected my key at the concierge's desk I found he had a message for me, too.

"A gentleman is waiting to see you in the Bar Anglais, Monsieur Carter."

"A gentleman?" I repeated. "Did he leave his name? Can you describe him?"

He shrugged apologetically. "I'm sorry, Monsieur, but he arrived before I came on duty. That is all the information I have. If you like, I can have them page the bar and ask for—"

"No," I said, cutting him off. "Thanks, but that won't be necessary." Very few people knew I was staying at the Plaza Athénée and I wasn't expecting any of them. At least I wouldn't have far to go to find out who it was. The Bar Anglais was one floor below the main lobby.

"I've got to meet someone," I informed Lauren. She'd stopped off at the newsstand for a pack of *Disque Bleu* and had missed my conversation with the concierge.

"Am I included in the invitation?"

"No, you're not." I said it in a hard, firm tone that implied we weren't going to debate the issue.

She looked at me, letting the silence build for a few seconds. "Okay," she said finally. "I'll go up to the room and wait for you. Not that I *need* the practice. Unless you've already forgotten, I spent most of the day doing just that."

"This is business, Lauren." I pressed the key in her hand. I wanted to say more, to try and explain to her just what was at stake. But I forced myself not to.

In the espionage business caring too much is just another bad habit, like excessive smoking or drinking. A little indulgence is good for you, but go beyond that and you lose the edge that keeps you on top. I knew I was beyond the "reasonable" point with Lauren and now was the time to draw the line. "Don't wait up for me," I said with the widest smile I could muster. "I may not be back until sometime tomorrow. If you should get restless, you can go back to your apartment. I think it's safe enough now."

"I'll keep that in mind," she said in a near whisper. "But before you go, there's something I want to tell you. When I saw Agabar's body, I wasn't shocked. A little upset maybe, but that was about it. I'm starting to get *used* to seeing people die. And even worse than that, I'm starting to get used to *you*."

It was a good exit line and that's what she used it for. I watched her cross the lobby in long, graceful strides, her head held high and defiant. I wasn't quite sure what to make of her parting re-marks. They were sufficiently cryptic to let her do whatever she wanted and still have the satisfaction of having "told me off."

I hadn't been lying when I'd said it was safe for her to go back to her apartment. But I hadn't ex-actly been telling the truth either. There was still a strong possibility that her life was in danger, espe-cially now that she'd been seen with me at the re-ception. But I also knew that I'd be moving too fast during the next few days to give her the kind of protection she needed. Any field agent could do the job better simply because that was *all* he'd have to do.

I used one of the lobby pay phones to make the arrangements and then took the elevator down to the Bar Anglais.

As the name implies it is an "English bar," a bit of the other side of the Channel right here in the heart of Paris. And they'd done a proper job of it, with dark wood paneling, comfortable leather armchairs, and a Scottish tartan rug.

There must have been a shortage of homesick Anglos because the place was nearly deserted to-night. I paused in the doorway and let my eyes wander around the room. Two salesman types in animated conversation, a tourist party of four, and a bored but beautiful "lady of the night." Even in the best hotels they can't keep them out. I've always had a suspicion that they don't really want to.

I was beginning to think that my nameless friend

had given up and gone home, when I noticed a thin blue spiral of smoke rising above one of the chairs in the back of the room. No one else appeared to be anxiously awaiting *Monsieur* Carter, so I decided that it was worth walking over just to make sure.

I passed the prostitute on the way. She quickly worked up a warm smile for me, along with a meaningful glance from the deepest amber eyes I'd ever seen. There was nothing cheap about her; in fact, her simple-looking beige skirt and jacket were the work of one of the city's top couturiers. I know, because I'd seen the exact same outfit while shopping with Lauren that afternoon. That, along with the diamond earrings she was wearing, would have put me back almost three months' pay. I shook my head—regretfully, I hope, because she really was stunning—and continued on toward the back of the room.

I smelled him before I saw him. Or rather, I should say I smelled *it*. There's only one person in the world I know who smokes those God-awful, foul-smelling cigars.

My boss, David Hawk.

I circled around the high, winged-back chair for my first look at him in more than three weeks. I'd finished a job in Italy before this assignment and hadn't expected to see Hawk until I was back in the States.

"I hope you're not surprised," his raspy voice greeted me. "Because surprise is an element I like to reserve almost exclusively for the other side. If you follow my meaning, Nick?"

"Yes, sir. I do." Hawk had always said that a Killmaster should be ready for anything and always expect the unexpected. The "other side" he referred to was a catchall term for whomever we happened to be fighting at the moment—Russians, Chinese, Baader-Meinhof, PLO. Sometimes the names changed so fast I couldn't keep track of them all.

"Sit down," he said, nodding toward the vacant chair across from him. "It's good to see you again, Nick, but I wish it were under different circumstances."

I looked at him without speaking. The last part of what he'd just said gave me a cold, uncomfortable feeling all the way down my spine. The director of a super-secret intelligence agency like AXE doesn't fly clear across the Atlantic merely to see how you're getting along. On those rare occasions when he does leave his desk, it's usually to pull someone *off* an assignment.

Why? Because he's not good enough anymore.

Hawk fixed me with his flinty eyes and smiled. "I can tell by the look on your face what you're thinking, Nick. And I'm happy to say you're wrong. My presence in Paris isn't a reflection on your performance so far, but rather on the gravity of the situation."

"I have a feeling there's something that I don't know about yet."

"Yes," he said quietly. "And it isn't welcome news. The customs officials made an interesting discovery this morning out at Charles de Gaulle Airport. A transport plane in from New York was off-loading a cargo of fifty-five gallon drums. The drums were marked and invoiced "industrial solvents," but when a fork-lift backed into one by accident, the lid came off and the contents spilled out on the tarmac. What it was," he concluded in a grim voice, "was fifty-five gallons of RXD packed in gel. And the other twenty-nine drums contained exactly the same thing."

RXD. The initials sounded harmless until you found out what they stood for—*cylotrimethylene trinitramine,* one of the most lethal and unstable *plastiques* ever made. In fact, it's so dangerous to transport that it's been categorized as a Class-A explosive, making it illegal to ship on any kind of plane.

It was only pure luck that the accident didn't result in a massive explosion. The amount of RXD Hawk was talking about could have taken apart the entire airport.

"That's only the first part of the story," Hawk continued. "After they made the discovery, the French very wisely allowed the drums to be delivered to their destination. Of course, they weren't the *original* drums," he added with a dry chuckle, "but the best substitutes they could come up with on short notice. Two Mercedes trucks picked up the bogus cargo at one and drove it about one hundred kilometers south of Paris to a town called Étréchy. Their destination was an auto parts warehouse just outside the town limits. Naturally, the customs and internal security people tailed them from the airport, and when the delivery men started unloading, they moved in."

"And found?" I couldn't help asking, even though I was fairly certain I wasn't going to like the answer.

"A nearly empty warehouse. I know that doesn't sound particularly frightening," Hawk said in response to my puzzled expression, "but believe me, Nick, it *is*. There were just enough items left to clearly indicate what had been going on. Those items included a Redeye missile, a case of M-16's, radio monitors, infrared night vision scopes, encoding devices, and thermite pencils. I think you see what I'm driving at?"

"A clearing house," I said softly. The implications of what Hawk had been telling me were just starting to come together in my mind. The total effect was devastating.

"Exactly so," said Hawk with a grim nod. "The auto-parts cover was perfect for shipping weapons all over the country. And from the look of all the dismantled packing crates and such, enough 'hardware' must have passed through there to outfit a couple of small armies. What the French found was probably the last lot waiting to be shipped out with the RXD. There was no one at the warehouse and the truck drivers clearly didn't know what was going on. Their instructions were simple: pick up, deliver, and unload. They were well-paid for it in advance."

Hawk paused a moment to relight his mangled-looking cigar. "The problem is that we don't know where any of it went. The French looked over the trucking company's records, which show that they've been hauling similar loads of cargo to the warehouse in Étréchy for more than a year now. Where it went from there is anyone's guess, although I'm sure it's still in the country. Otherwise, why all the elaborate smuggling if they intended to ship it elsewhere?"

That was a good point, but also a disconcerting one. Arms had been pouring into France for over a year and still none of them had surfaced yet. Someone was stockpiling with something more than just a little sniping in mind. The capabilities of some of the items Hawk had listed made my blood run cold.

The Redeye was a prime example. It's a small shoulder-launching missile with its own heat-seeking device. Anyone with minimal training and a Redeye could wipe out a 747 in midair.

"Did the French find anything that links it to the diplomatic assassinations?" .

Through a cloud of swirling cigar smoke, I watched Hawk shake his head. "Instinct," he said quietly. "That's really what I'm going on. The assassinations and the arms smuggling are both the work of professionals, *top* professionals, I might add. We'd be foolish to think that there *wasn't* some connection between the two operations. Now that you know the worst of it," he concluded with a wintry smile, "bring me up to date on your own activities."

Over a couple of glasses of vintage Armagnac, I did just that. Hawk listened patiently, his cool, appraising eyes never leaving me. Maybe it was only jet-lag, but he looked tired almost to the point of exhaustion. His stern face was drawn and pale, and his slender shoulders looked as though they had the weight of the world on them.

Hell. Neither one of us was getting any younger. Still, I was glad Hawk had come to Paris, even with the bad news that had brought him here. If things started getting hairy, and I was sure they would, he was the one man in the world I knew I could rely on.

"Where were the three possibles?" Hawk interrupted me. I'd just finished telling him about Agabar's murder. Of course, the "three possibles" were Gail, Christine, and Ann-Marie.

"Nowhere near the body. Not that that makes any difference," I quickly added. "Agabar was probably killed right after he made his little speech about the lights. The assassin used the sound of his voice to locate him in the dark. It was fairly easy to predict that he'd make some kind of announcement concerning the blackout. But the lights didn't come back on until roughly three minutes after he finished speaking. Plenty of time for the assassin to put a lot of distance between herself and the body."

"You still say 'herself,' implying that you continue to regard these three women as our principal suspects." He paused and looked down thoughtfully at his smoldering cigar. "I don't want to start second-guessing you," he said, meeting my eyes again, "but if you're wrong, Nick, the consequences could be disastrous."

"The Arab oil summit?"

"Precisely. Whoever this terrorist group is, they obviously have an intense hatred for former colonies, Third World countries—any emerging nation ruled by *nonwhites*. So far they've murdered five diplomats, not a large number when you think of it. But then, many of these countries only have a small percentage of the population with the education and abilities for these top government jobs. They're not just killing people," Hawk said harshly, "they're trying to wipe out a country's *future*. And with all the tension in the Middle East," he concluded, "I don't see how they could pass up the oil summit."

"I'm sure it's one of the three, sir," I said as confidently as I possibly could. It didn't bother me that Hawk questioned my judgment. That was part of his job as director of AXE—to probe and poke at our theories, to look at the reasons behind each decision. Only this time I had next to nothing to offer him. Possibilities, coincidences, suspicions. But not one thing strong enough to clearly identify our assassin and the organization she worked for.

With her handy home arsenal, Gail Huntington was far and away the front runner. But it still didn't sit right with me. There was something *else* there, something else I couldn't quite put my finger on.

"It's getting late," Hawk said, rising wearily from the chair. He flipped open his worn cowhide wallet and dropped a couple of bills on the table. "You'd better wait about ten minutes and then go upstairs. It's all right if we're seen together, but there's no point in taking unnecessary risks."

"Where are you staying, sir?"

"Right down the hall from you. So if Lauren is still there, try not to keep me awake all night."

With a cynical parting smile, he turned and walked out of the bar.

Chapter Thirteen

"I know where they are," André Boissier said.

"You're positive?"

He nodded his massive head and grinned. "And that's not even the best part of it, *mon ami*. The information isn't going to cost you a single franc."

It was ten the next morning and I was back at Le Rénard Rouge. As just like my previous visit, the chairs were still stacked up on the tables, the calvados flowcd freely, and Boissier looked like he had the great-grandmother of all hangovers.

"It usually doesn't work that way," he continued, "but my informant happens to be someone who owes me *le grand faveur*. So I was able to secure this for you without any money changing hands."

"You're entitled to the ten thousand," I said reasonably. "It isn't coming out of my pocket, André."

I usually don't try and *give* AXE money away. But in view of the long-standing friendship between Boissier and Hawk, I felt I had to make some effort. All it did was make Boissier angry.

"You don't understand," he roared. "It isn't a matter of money. I'm happy to do it for my old comrade in arms, for David. I guess I'm just sentimental. Like senility, it comes with old age."

He probably was, but glaring down at me with those bloodshot eyes he looked about as sentimental as a Kodiak bear on the rampage.

"I know he'll appreciate it," I assured him. "Not to mention my own thanks."

That calmed him down enough to pour us both another shot of calvados. He tossed his glass back in a single gulp and wiped his grizzled red beard with the back of his hand.

"Do you know Vitry?" he asked, leaning closer. I was glad we had the bar between us. His breath smelled like a badly run distillery.

"Yes," I admitted, "but I've only driven through it a couple of times." It was one of those places you only visited if you had to. Vitry was a shabby working-class neighborhood on the outskirts of the city, a part of what the French called the "red belt," a ring of proletarian Communist enclaves surrounding Paris. If you really wanted to spend a depressing day, Vitry was the perfect place to do it in.

"This is the address," Boissier continued. "I don't think you'll have much trouble locating it. It's right off the main thoroughfare, Rue du Bois."

He pushed a scrap of paper across the scarred mahogany bar. Printed on it in clumsy block letters were the words and numbers 14 Rue de la Croix.

Street of the cross. For a moment I wondered if there might be something prophetic in the name. I folded the piece of paper up and tucked it away in the breast pocket of my tweed jacket. I'd already memorized the information, but I was still very curious about Boissier's anonymous tipster. If the note was in his handwriting, it was worth hanging onto for awhile.

"Any idea what kind of a building it is?" I asked. "Or how big a welcoming committee I'm going to find there?"

"No, *mon ami.*" He shrugged his broad shoulders and poured out more calvados. "All I know is that's where the terrorist group is operating from. The same ones responsible for the diplomatic assassinations. Now drink up," he said, clapping me on the back. "I don't want you driving on an empty stomach."

It wasn't exactly the best advice in the world, but I drained my glass anyway. The sharp apple brandy had a real kick to it. It warmed my insides, reminding me of Lauren and another kind of warmth. She'd been waiting for me when I'd gone up to the room last night. I hadn't spoken to Hawk this morning, so I didn't know whether we'd kept him awake or not.

If I had, I knew I was going to hear about it.

Just as I reached Vitry, the slate gray sky opened up and the rain began drumming out a message on the roof of the Renault. I flicked on my lights and wipers and slowed down to a crawl as I tried to read the street signs. The rain didn't help any. I hadn't been expecting it and had left my trench coat back at the hotel. I should have known better. After all, this was Vitry.

I'd decided the Ferrari was a bit too conspicuous for this neighborhood, so I'd rented a Renault two-door and left the 512 Boxer in the safekeeping of the hotel garage. I'd tried to contact Hawk before I'd left, but he wasn't in his room and hadn't left any messages for me with the concierge.

Since it was my decision, I elected to make this a solo operation for two reasons. One, because AXE's manpower in the Paris area was already overextended. Last night, Hawk had assigned tails to all three of my "lovely" ladies and dispatched another team to try and trace the weapons flow from the warehouse in Étréchy.

And second, I worked better alone. I could reconnoiter the sight and see what there was to see. If it turned out to be a false alarm, at least no one else would have wasted any time on it. And if it *were* the real thing, I could always call in a backup team.

Vitry's streets were long, straight, and boring. They were lined with shabby-looking stores, garages, and whole blocks of off-white apartment houses that looked like they'd started falling apart before construction was even finished. Because of the dark sky and heavy morning rain, the sodium street lamps were on. Their pale, glowing light made everything look just that much more grimy and neglected.

I finally found the Rue de la Croix. I parked and

locked the rental car, then walked another two blocks with the rain seeping down my upturned collar. There was no one in the street except for three skinny boys kicking a soccer ball around a vacant lot. But I could feel a hundred eyes watching me from behind the dirt-streaked windows overlooking the street. This was not a neighborhood that welcomed strangers.

I walked by number 14 deliberately, only allowing myself a quick, casual glance at the building itself. The sign above the stable-like doors was lopsided and warped from too many years of service. In peeling red and gold paint it spelled out the legend: CIRQUE DE HIVER, which translated into "winter circus." The smells had stayed behind, but I was pretty sure that the circus had packed up the elephants and left town a long time ago.

I continued around the block and down the street running parallel to the back of the building. By now I was soaked to the skin, my tweed jacket and tan slacks wrinkled and dripping. The only solace was that it made me blend in a little better with my surroundings.

About midway down the block, I ducked in an alleyway. If my calculations were correct, it should have been leading me right up to the back of number 14. The alleyway dead-ended into a tall, wooden fence. I shimmied over the top, ripping my jacket in the process, and landed in a narrow courtyard.

I recognized the silhouette of the circus building. Now that I was where I wanted to be, all I had to do was figure out what to do next.

The back of the place looked even more dilapidated than the front: a single steel door with a broken cage-light over it and a rusty fire escape that ran all the way up to a dormer-style fire door on the roof. The roof itself was a sloping mansard affair covered with rotting gray shingles. There was a skylight at the top, but I doubted if I could reach it without breaking my neck.

I decided my best bet was the fire door. The rust-pocked iron stairs creaked and groaned under my weight. They were slippery from the rain and I had to hold onto the railing with both hands or risk losing my footing. If someone had started shooting at me then, there wouldn't have been much I could do about it.

I finally made it to the top. The fire door looked like it hadn't been opened in years, but on the other hand there didn't seem to be any kind of lock on it. I twisted the knob and pulled. Nothing.

I braced my feet against the door and gave it a real tug. The knob came off in my hand and my momentum carried me back against the railing and almost over it. But at the last second my hand locked around a slippery iron rung and I saved myself from a forty-foot drop down to the concrete courtyard.

I'd managed to hang on to the knob, too. Not knowing what else to do with it, I slipped it inside my jacket pocket.

It was time to try a different approach on the door. I used the screwdriver blade on my pocket knife, working it gently but firmly back and forth along the opening between the door and the frame. When I'd loosened things up a bit, I put more leverage on it. The fire door popped open with a sharp metallic sound that was muffled by the falling rain.

I eased Wilhelmina free of my shoulder holster and moved cautiously forward into total darkness. I reached out with my other hand and touched dirt-encrusted canvas. A cobweb broke over my face and all around me I could smell years and years of accumulated dust. I was walking along a narrow wooden board, which wasn't the easiest thing to do in the dark—especially when you don't have the slightest idea where it's taking you.

After about fifteen feet, I saw a dim, murky light up ahead. As I got closer I also saw what I'd been walking along: the top tier in a set of bleachers that slanted steeply down to a small circus ring some forty feet below. At one time this had probably been the off-season home of some third- or fourth-rate traveling circus and carnival show.

There were still a few remnants of the former tenants—a broken trapeze rig dangling from the ceiling; a herd of wooden carousel horses stacked against the wall, their sleek lines obliterated by a blanket of dust; and, down in the ring, a unicycle with its huge wheel twisted out of shape.

The clowns and high flyers were long gone, but the place was far from empty.

I counted seventeen men and women. The shadows could have held twice as many more, but that was all I could see from my vantage point. They were dressed paramilitary style in a mixture of khaki, olive drab, and jungle camouflage jackets and trousers. None of them looked alike except in two respects: they were all white and they were all carrying Russian-made Kalashnikov Assault Rifles.

They were sitting around in small groups, some talking, some reading, while others just held onto their rifles and tried to look tough. The acoustics were rotten. I couldn't hear anything more than a few disjointed words. But from the pitch and timbre of the voices, I was sure they were English-speaking. The majority of the group had deeply tanned skin with the kind of ruddiness that usually means a British Isles or Northern European background.

Of course, it was all guesswork on my part, but I thought I knew who they were—Rhodesian or South African terrorists.

They certainly looked the part. And their white supremacist politics and strong commitment to the colonial lifestyle were the perfect opposite to the views held by the five murdered diplomats.

Naturally, like any theory, it had its holes—the biggest one being, what were they doing in France? They'd see a lot more action right on their own home front. So why were they hanging around an abandoned circus when they should have been out patrolling the bush? I'm sure they applauded the assassinations, but they didn't do much to further their *spécifique* cause.

The other hole was that I didn't see any of my three suspects among the half-dozen women present. Still, she might walk in any second with her AXE tail right behind her. It was a comforting thought, but I didn't want to start indulging in daydreams just yet.

Instead, I put Wilhelmina away and sat down on the bleachers to watch the show. I'd seen more than a hundred groups like this one, small, dedicated, fanatical. Half of them joined just because they had some half-assed romantic image of themselves centered around battle fatigues and a gun.

Don't get me wrong, though, I took them very seriously. Too many times I'd seen what a well-armed group that size can do in the way of death and destruction.

For the moment they seemed to be merely biding their time. I decided to do the same. As soon as the rain let up, I would sneak back out and call in a backup team. We'd be able to take most of them alive, at least I hoped so. After a few hours with the interrogation specialists, I was sure that any of the survivors would be more than happy to tell us the identity of the embassy hit woman.

I was beginning to shiver in my sodden clothes. I felt like having a cigarette, but I couldn't risk attracting anyone's attention. If I could wrap this up this afternoon, I'd probably be able to squeeze a week's leave out of Hawk before he sent me chasing to some other hot-spot halfway round the globe.

I already knew what I'd do with it—spend it

right here in Paris with Lauren. Long, rich, gourmet meals and long, rich, gourmet nights in bed.

Someone down below must have been psychic, because two of the women put down their Kalashnikovs and began to pass out lunch. Everyone got the same thing: a small bottle of wine, a sandwich wrapped in wax paper, and a candy bar for dessert. I suddenly realized how hungry I had become.

I was considering going down and asking for just one bite when a massive explosion sent me hurtling into oblivion.

Chapter Fourteen

It was trying to kill me—the *it* being a thick, swirling, greenish-gray fog that had me pinned to the wall like a butterfly on a velvet board. I couldn't move my arms or legs and the pressure against my chest was going to split it wide open in a few more seconds.

The fog filled my mouth and lungs, leaving me gasping for air. I tried to fight it off, but nothing I did seemed to help. Someone had severed the line of communications between my body and my brain. I was paralyzed, defenseless, and about to die.

Hands reached out of the fog to taunt me, long, slender hands with carmine-tipped nails. They stayed just out of reach, with whatever they were connected to hidden somewhere deep in the smoky mist.

Just as I was about to go under, the fog began to recede, slowly at first and then quickly, as if a great rush of wind had blown it all away. I blinked my eyes and started fighting my way back into the real world. The wall I'd been pinned against was actually the floor of the circus building. And the sinister, choking fog was nothing more than the years of accumulated dust the explosion had unsettled.

I remembered about the explosion now. I was obviously doing fine. But for a while—I still didn't know how long—I'd been out of it, lost in some other place halfway between dream and reality.

The nightmare quality of it left me with a cold, uneasy feeling. My helplessness and the beckoning hands seemed like messages from my subconscious. They had been very feminine hands. One or all of my suspects? Whatever I'd been trying to tell myself, I hadn't gotten the message across very well.

I'd already wasted enough time on my mind; it was time to check out the Carter body. I felt stiff all over. I tried to push myself up from the floor and a wave of pain brought me right back down again.

I sucked in air and gave it another shot. This time it wasn't nearly as bad and I managed to make it up to a sitting position. My arms and legs felt numb, but with slow, gradual movement they began to limber up.

Even though I'd survived, I probably didn't look it. I needed a mirror to assess the damage to my face, but the rest of me was singed, dirty, and ragged beyond recognition. There were cuts and abrasions on my chest and arms and a nasty gash below my right knee. I also had the familiar taste of blood in my mouth. Apart from that I was the same old indestructable Nick.

The others hadn't been as lucky. Rising awkwardly to my feet, I looked around at the carnage: bodies burned and mangled so badly that they no longer looked human, severed limbs and that sweet-sick odor that would hang in the air even after they'd been carted away in plastic body bags. It was the kind of death that made you glad there were no survivors.

I'd been too far away to get the full impact of the explosion. From the force and the blasting pattern, it looked as if *plastique* had been used. Possibly an earlier shipment of RXD from the warehouse in Étréchy?

Working with something that unstable, they could have easily caused the explosion themselves. If not, then who did? Ever since I'd started this assignment, I seemed to be winding up with two new questions for each answer I found. Miraculously, my AXE issue watch had also survived the blast. It was only eleven-twenty. Less than an hour and a half since I'd left Boissier's cafe. It really seemed like a hell of a way to start the morning.

I walked up a splintered staircase and out the back door. In the distance I could hear the urgent wail of sirens. They were becoming so familiar now, I almost couldn't imagine Paris without them.

Naturally, since this was Vitry it was raining harder than ever.

Chapter Fifteen

"It looks like a map of the Russian front," the doctor observed with a wry smile.

He was talking about my body, which he'd just finished ministering to. In the process he'd patched me up in about seventeen different places, topping each one off with a thick layer of gauze and bandages. He'd also determined that there were no bones broken and that I'd be fine after a few days of total rest.

"Rest," he repeated, "that's the best thing I can prescribe for you. Your wounds aren't severe, but your body has had a tremendous shock. I can't take responsibility for what might happen if you don't follow my advice."

"I'll bear that in mind," I told him.

I guess I didn't sound very convincing, because he scowled at me and snapped his black bag shut as if he were anxious to collect his fee and return to the company of more *sensible* people who actually took his advice.

He was a tall, cadaverous-looking old geezer

with water gray eyes and a white Van Dyke beard. I never found out his name or where Hawk had gotten him from. He certainly wasn't the hotel doctor. That would have involved too many unnecessary and embarrassing questions.

When he left my bedside, Lauren took his place. She'd been hovering over me ever since I'd returned to my room by way of the hotel's service entrance. Since I might want to stay at the Plaza Athénée again some time, I figured it was the least I could do.

"Comfortable?" Lauren asked. She put a cool hand on my cheek and then leaned down to kiss me. Suddenly, I was feeling a whole lot better.

"I'm fine," I said, pulling her down next to me. She let out a gasp of protest, but quickly settled into my arms, her long, supple body molding itself to mine.

I was just about to start laying the groundwork for my own best prescription when someone knocked at the door. Not exactly what you'd call perfect timing.

"It's probably Hawk," I told her, "and don't forget to button up that blouse before you answer it."

"Cochon," she cursed me, grinning.

As she crossed the room, I picked up my Luger from the bedside table. I was fairly sure it was Hawk who'd arranged to pay off the doctor and who was now probably stopping by to see how I was doing. But then the way things had been going, I didn't want to take any chances.

"I hope I didn't interrupt anything," Hawk's gruff voice greeted me from the open door. "But it's imperative that we talk."

"No, come on in," I told him.

Lauren's face had turned a bright red when Hawk had said "interrupt," but she greeted him cordially and even went so far as to pull a chair up to the bed for him. They'd met earlier over my battered body and I think she wasn't quite sure what to make of him yet.

"I have some things to attend to," she announced diplomatically. "I'll come and look in on you later, Nick." She strode into the adjoining room and closed the door firmly behind her.

"Intelligent girl," Hawk commented. "Now tell me, do you feel up to handling the rest of this mission?"

"Yes," I answered truthfully. "I may not be able to move as fast as I usually do, but other than that I should be fine."

"Good," he said curtly, "because I think we both know it would be impossible to replace you at this point in the game. I don't know what I'd have done if you'd died in that explosion."

If I hadn't known Hawk as long as I did, I might have thought that last part was a bit cold. But Hawk isn't cold so much as logical. We had a job to do and there was a lot more at stake than one man's life.

"Now tell me what happened," Hawk continued, "and don't leave out any details."

My report took almost two hours, covering

everything from Boissier's phone call right up to the moment I collapsed on the hotel bed. Probably out of deference to my health, he only smoked one of his famous "El Defecto" cigars. When I finished the recital he looked none too happy.

"What do you think?" he asked abruptly.

I shook my head. "It still doesn't make any sense to me. I really don't see what any terrorist group would hope to accomplish by murdering five different diplomats from five different countries. I realize that they're important men, but they're not heads of state. None of their deaths are going to throw their countries into a revolutionary turmoil. There just doesn't seem to be any point to it, sir. And that," I added, "is what's been bothering me ever since I started this assignment."

Hawk nodded agreement. "That's true enough, but many of these radical groups assassinate people just for the publicity value, the media exposure they're so sure of getting in this age of instant communications."

"Then why hasn't anyone claimed the credit?" I countered.

Hawk was saved from answering by the phone. He picked it up on the first ring, grunted hello, and listened intently to what my caller had to say.

"You'd better get dressed," he said, hanging up the receiver. "Gail Huntington is on her way out of Paris, and according to her tail, she's heavily armed."

Chapter Sixteen

"Come in, N3, come in."

Through the crackle and static I recognized Jake Talbert's voice. He was the field agent who'd taken over the Huntington surveillance job after Steve Woodriss had died.

I scooped up the receiver with my free hand and said, "This is N3. Go ahead; I read you."

"Subject is now parked outside a cottage on the Place Napoleon Bonaparte, two blocks south of the Hotel de L'Aigle Noir. Instructions?"

"Sit tight," I told him. "I know your location and should be there in about fifteen minutes. Over and out."

I returned all my attention back to the road. I was on the main highway heading south toward Lyon, the Ferrari humming along at a steady eighty miles per hour. Rolling hills, farmland, and industrial complexes merged into one long shadow outlined by the last rays of the setting sun. Traffic was sparse and because of the Ferrari's speed capabilities, I was less than a quarter of an hour behind Jake and the girl.

He'd radioed me once before when Gail's silver Mercedes sedan turned off at the exit for Fontainebleau. It's one of the prettiest towns in France with its château, gardens, and fifty thousand acres of forest that were once the private hunting preserve of the country's monarchs. I knew the hotel Jake had mentioned. I'd eaten an excellent *saucisson de homard* there about three years ago.

The only unanswered question was what was Gail doing in Fontainebleau that required a .357 and a Dragunov automatic rifle. Jake had seen her put both weapons in the car before she left Paris. Not in the trunk, but on the front seat where they were in easy reach.

Of course, the obvious solution was that Gail Huntington and our lady assassin were one and the same. But that still didn't quite hang together right. The embassy killing had been done by someone with exceptional tradecraft. If it were indeed Gail, then why hadn't she bothered to conceal the gun and rifle? It was an elementary precaution, something you'd expect even the rawest recruit to do.

I shifted uncomfortably in the low-slung leather seat, trying to find a position that minimized the pain. It was a hopeless task and I gave it up when I saw the Fontainebleau exit just ahead on my right.

I nosed the 512 down the off ramp and passed through the quiet town at a respectable thirty-five mph. The Hotel de L'Aigle Noir was directly across from the château. I cut the engine after I passed it and glided another hundred feet until the car was in the deep shadow of a plane tree.

Further down the block, I saw Talbert's Renault and beyond that, pulled up in front of a thatched-roof cottage, Gail's silver Mercedes.

Night had fallen and a strong breeze rustled the leaves of the plane tree. Overhead, a full moon was obscured by clouds. Staying deep in the shadows, I worked my way over to Talbert's car.

Jake nodded a silent hello as I slipped in beside him. "We've got company, Nick, further up the road on the other side."

My eyes turned in the direction he was pointing and I saw the dim outline of a compact car, a Datsun or Toyota probably. It was too dark for me to be sure.

"There're two men in it," Talbert continued. "I sneaked up for a closer look about ten minutes ago. They're just sitting there pretending to be invisible. Which isn't easy," he added with a soft chuckle, "because one of them keeps lighting a cigarette about every five minutes."

As if on cue, I saw a pinpoint of light flare up. A half-second later the compact was dark again.

"At least we're not dealing with pros," I observed. "Any other activity?"

"*Nada.* I got a feeling the party isn't complete yet. Otherwise, what's everyone still sitting around in cars for?"

I'd come to that same conclusion myself. There was an air of expectancy about this setup, in fact about the whole damn assignment, that was starting to get on my nerves. I wanted to *do* something for a change. In every encounter so far, I'd been reacting rather than acting. It seemed as though the enemy was always one step ahead of me. And, like the taunting hands in my dream, just out of reach.

"I'm going to scout around," I said casually.

Talbert shot me a quizzical glance and then turned his eyes back to the Mercedes. He was a big, broad-shouldered guy with the battered face of an ex-boxer. He looked like the kind of man you'd expect to find working as a bouncer in a second-rate Paris nightclub. That's why he made such a good field operative. Few people ever realized that there was a hundred-forty IQ behind that rough-and-tumble exterior.

I got out of the car and stretched. My muscles were stiff and sore; although the pain had eased up a bit, I knew I wouldn't be functioning anywhere near top form tonight.

I scrambled down into a shallow drainage ditch and began to work my way toward the compact. I'd only gone a few feet when I heard a car door slam. Like a reflex action, Wilhelmina filled my hand.

I turned toward the source of the noise and saw Gail heading for the cottage. The moon had come out from behind the clouds, its light accenting her soft, shining hair and the straight hard line of the Dragunov nestled in the crook of her arm.

Talbert crawled down the embankment and landed beside me. "She's going inside," he whispered. In the darkness I could see the outline of a Colt Cobra .38. Like myself, Jake had decided it was time to get his gun out.

"I saw her," I whispered back. "I'm going to move in as close as I can to the cottage. I want you to do the same for our two friends in the car. Just keep an eye on them for now. If they start anything," I paused and grinned at him, "use your own good judgment."

Jake nodded silent understanding. Staying in a low crouch, I moved along the ditch until I was opposite the cottage. I crawled back up the embankment and parted the high grass for a better view. There was a light in the cottage window now, a warm steady glow behind the net curtains.

I glanced over at the other side of the road. I thought I saw Jake weaving in and out of the shadow pools, but I really couldn't be sure. For such a big man, he moved with surprising grace and speed.

I was about thirty feet from the cottage now, about as close as I was going to get without the risk of being spotted. There was no cover any closer in, just a freshly mown lawn sloping down to the embankment and a graveled driveway that ran from the street to the cottage.

I settled into the tall grass and weeds and waited for something to happen. Waiting is an integral part of my trade, but I can't say I enjoy it. My main objection is that it gives you too much time to think, too much time to remember. If you're trying to figure something out, you start second-guessing yourself. And if you start thinking about the past, there always seems to be more bad to remember than good.

The luminous hands of my watch were positioned at exactly eight o'clock when I heard the sound of a car turning into the street. Only ten minutes had passed since Gail had entered the cottage.

The quiet purr of the engine grew louder and I turned just in time to see a sleek black Daimler swing into the driveway. Spraying gravel in its wake, it came to a stop behind the Mercedes. The running lights went out, but not before I caught a glimpse of the license tag on the rear bumper. It wasn't an ordinary plate, but a specially lettered one issued only to members of the diplomatic community.

I'd been wrong. It wasn't the first time, not that that made me feel any better. All too clearly I remembered telling Hawk last night that Gail Huntington just didn't fit in with my profile of the assassain. Now I had the girl, the gun, and what was probably a diplomat right under my nose. Unless there was some other explanation, my evaluation of Gail had been way off the mark.

The driver's side door of the Daimler opened and a tall figure stepped out onto the gravel. His back was to me so that all I really saw was a charcoal gray overcoat with the collar turned up and a black Homburg hat. His gloved right hand was wrapped around the handle of an attaché case. He closed the car door, extinguishing the interior light, and walked slowly up to the cottage.

"Entrez." It was Gail's voice that issued the one-word invitation. The door opened just wide enough to admit him and the Daimler man slipped inside.

I would have liked to have given them some time alone, just a minute or two to see what would happen, but I couldn't risk the possibility of another dead diplomat.

Even before the door started to close, I was on my feet and running. Each step sent a shock wave through my battered body. It was almost shut when I hit the sturdy oak planks. The door gave way under the impact of my shoulder and I hurled my way into the room in a low crouch.

A gunshot chipped away at the whitewashed wall just above my head. I brought the Luger around in an arc and squeezed the trigger.

Gail Huntington screamed as the bullet tore into her shoulder. The two hands clutching the Magnum began to convulse and then the long-barreled gun fell to the floor with a clatter.

I swung Wilhelmina toward the other side of the room where the Daimler man was bringing a Walther PPK into the action.

"Drop it," I ordered, "I'm here to save your ass, not waste it."

His hazel eyes mirrored confusion and I hastily repeated the command in French. He leaned over and put the automatic down on the flagstone floor. His other hand kept a tight grip on the brown leather attaché, holding it close to his side as if he were afraid I was going to make a grab for it.

With my Luger still aimed at his chest, I collected the two handguns and slipped them through my belt. I had to look for the Dragunov, but I quickly found the rifle propped up against the mantle where a broad band of shadow had kept it hidden but close at hand.

Gail was moaning softly now, her head bowed low so that her long chestnut hair spilled over her face like a mask. Her arms were wrapped around her knees in that same "little-girl-lost" position I'd left her in the day we made love. Blood flowed freely from the wound in her shoulder. For no reason that I could think of, I was glad I hadn't killed her.

A burst of machine-gun fire shattered the silence. I gave the Daimler man a meaningful glance. From the look on his face I knew he'd gotten my message: Don't try anything if you want to live.

I yanked open the cottage door and dove for cover. The machine gun stitched a ragged line across the mantle, shattering the mirror above into a shower of flying glass. I poked my head around the door frame and drew another furious blast. One thing was certain, I wasn't going to get in a shot from my present position.

Luckily, in my scramble for cover I'd landed on the window side of the cottage. It wasn't much of a spot for returning fire either, but it worked in well with the plan that had been forming in my mind.

I moved toward the window, pausing just long enough to pull the plug on the lamp that would have silhouetted me like a sitting duck. So much for the easy part. The rest of it depended on timing and *luck*.

I smashed a windowpane and squeezed off a single round. The answer was immediate, a barrage of heavy fire that left a huge jagged hole where my hand had just been. As bullets continued to pock the opposite wall, I raced back to the door and took aim.

The first shot hit Rodrigo in the face, shattering his cheek into a bloody eruption of flesh and bone. His mouth made an O of surprise as he fell forward, collapsing on top of the Stoner Light machine gun. A final spasm rippled his body before it settled into an awkward sprawl.

I couldn't be sure, but I think he'd seen me out of the corner of his eye during that frantic split second he'd tried to swing the Stoner back to the door. I'll never know for certain, but I hoped he had. That's how much I hated the man.

If Rodrigo had been one of the pair in the compact, then I had a feeling that Hector was his missing partner. Probably the smoker, I thought, remembering his heavy cigarette consumption the night I first saw him at the Agency Castel. But where was he, and, more importantly, where was Jake Talbert?

I glanced back at Gail and the Daimler man. She hadn't moved, but the shallow sound of her breathing told me she was still alive. The Daimler man was huddled in the corner, his dark gray topcoat streaked with dust. He'd lost his Homburg during the excitement, exposing a dome as pink and hairless as a baby's bottom. His wary brown eyes looked up at me and then quickly back to the floor.

Neither one of them was going anywhere. Gail couldn't run and Daimler looked too frightened to try it. I decided it was safe enough to leave them on their own for a minute or so.

I picked up the Russian-made sniper's rifle and stepped out into the cool night air. Now that the shooting had stopped the street seemed quiet, almost *too* quiet. There were no other dwellings nearby and the Hotel de L'Aigle Noir was far enough down the road so that the sound of the gunfire would have been fairly dimmed by the time it reached there. No one had called the *flics,* I reasoned. Otherwise they would have been here by now.

I worked my way toward the road, my eyes constantly scanning the moonlit landscape. I heard a rustling in a clump of bushes to my right and swung the Dragunov into firing position.

"Nick, don't shoot!"

Jake Talbert's voice was a welcome sound to my ears. I dipped the rifle toward the ground as he came staggering out of the bushes. His suit was torn in three places, the left sleeve dangling by a couple of threads. That, combined with his bruised and battered face, made him look the sole survivor of a train wreck.

"You okay?" I asked, hurrying up to meet him.

"I'm fine," he said, waving me back. "It just *looks* a lot worse than it really is. You should see the other guy." With a nod of his head he indicated the cluster of laurel bushes he had just emerged from.

At first I didn't see him. Then my eyes zeroed in on two feet projecting out of the shrubbery. Following the scuffed wingtips, I pushed aside the bushes and saw Hector stretched out on the ground, just as dead as his pal Rodrigo. The cause of death wasn't hard to guess. Jake's powerful hands had made a strong, lasting impression on the mestizo's bull neck.

"I was starting to worry about you," I said, hunkering down next to Jake. He was sitting on the grass now, using his tie to wipe the worst of the dirt from his face.

"So was I," he admitted, grinning. "I don't think I've ever taken on a tougher son of a bitch in hand-to-hand combat. It was real close there for a while, Nick."

"What exactly happened?"

"Well," Jake said with a sigh, "when the shooting started inside the cottage the two guys in the compact headed that way on the run. Both of them were armed with Stoners and I knew I couldn't take more than one on at a time without getting my butt blown off." He nodded toward the Colt Cobra lying beside him in the grass. The .38 wasn't exactly an even match for two lightweight machine guns.

"So I jumped the guy bringing up the rear. They were far enough apart so that the other one didn't hear him go down. I got the Stoner away from him and then we went to it." Talbert paused and shook his head in disbelief. "He didn't have much formal training but he sure put up one hell of a fight. By the time I finished him off, the shooting was over and you were out here looking for me. I guess I didn't do much of a job as a backup," he added dismally.

"You were great," I assured him. It was only a small lie and it would go a long way toward restoring his self-confidence. "I've got some unfinished business inside," I said, standing. "I don't think the gendarmes are going to be paying us a visit, but if you could tidy up the landscape a bit, we could both breathe a little easier."

"I'll get right on it," Jake said, pulling himself to his feet. I knew I could count on him to take care of the bodies and the car, and it would help take his mind off the way he'd handled the mestizos.

Walking back to the cottage, I couldn't help feeling a certain letdown myself. I hadn't exactly called all the shots right on this one. And even though I'd caught my lady assassin, it didn't give me much satisfaction. No matter how many different ways I fitted the pieces together, it still didn't make any sense. But then terrorism itself was senseless. I guess I'd just have to live with the fact that my instincts had been wrong for once.

"The good samaritan," I said softly. I had crossed the threshold to find the Daimler man leaning over Gail. He jumped at the sound of my voice and spun around.

"I was only trying to help," he said in heavily accented English. Maybe he was, but I hadn't seen eyes that guilty in a long time.

"Stand up," I said curtly. To hasten the process I prodded his spine with the barrel of the Dragunov.

He yelped and leaped into the center of the room like a child's spring-up toy. But even my little poke hadn't served to loosen his hold on the attaché. He clutched it to his chest as if it were the last life preserver on the Titanic.

"Put down the case," I demanded.

He shook his head uncertainly. "Diplomatic immunity," he explained in a choked whisper. "You cannot force me to do anything against my will. I'm completely protected by diplomatic immunity."

"Is that so," I said lightly. "Funny thing is, I don't see anyone else around here except you, me, and the girl. Now unless you want me to *blow* you apart from that case," I growled, "you'd better put it down on that table *now.*"

His eyes registered total fear. He started to say something and then changed his mind. With trembling hands he put the attaché down on the table.

"Open it," I snapped.

It took a while because his fingers were shaking too much to unlatch the twin gold clasps on the first couple of tries. Finally, he accomplished the task and raised the lid. Considering the contents, it had been worth the wait.

The attaché was packed solid with money. Thick, paper-banded bundles of United States currency. All of the notes on top were crisp new hundreds. Gauging the size of the case, there could be almost half a million there if the other bills were of the same denomination.

"Don't tell me," I said, smiling. "They're giving a waffle iron away with every new account at the local bank and you just couldn't pass up a bargain. Right?"

He looked more confused now than anything. "Waffle iron," he repeated slowly. His Middle-European accent was heavier than before.

"Never mind," I snarled with irritation. "Just tell me what you're doing with all that cash."

"A business transaction," he replied in a faltering voice. "Nothing that concerns you, *monsieur*. Merely a simple business deal I have undertaken on behalf of my government."

"And what kind of business does your government have with her?" With a curt nod I indicated the wounded girl propped up against the wall. This whole incident wasn't turning out anything like I thought it would. For openers, it was beginning to look less and lesser still like a setup for an assassination.

"I'd rather not go into that," he answered with a thin smile. "Obviously, it can't be concluded tonight, so if you don't mind I'll be on my way now." Confidence had returned to his voice and his hands barely trembled as he snapped the attaché shut and picked it up from the table. But if he thought I was going to let him just walk away without an explanation, then he was clearly overdue for a trip to *Fantasy Island*.

"You're blocking the door, *monsieur*."

For a diplomat this guy really had an eye for detail. I leaned the rifle against the wall and grabbed a double-handful of the Daimler man's coat. Suddenly I was feeling *very* undiplomatic.

"Talk to me," I growled, slamming him against the wall. "And if you say 'diplomatic immunity' or 'business transaction' just once, I'm going to knock your teeth down your throat."

His head bobbed up and down in frantic agreement. It was nice to know we'd finally found a way to communicate. His shoulders began to sag and I gave him a gentle shove, just enough to keep him standing.

We both looked down in response to the thumping noise.

The blue plastic bag had landed at my feet. I looked up and saw the corner of its mate protruding from Daimler's overcoat pocket. It seemed I had shaken something more than words out of him.

With one hand I kept him pinned to the wall while I used the other to extract the second bag. It wasn't light; close to a pound, I guessed, hefting it in my outstretched palm.

I scooped the other one up from the floor and carried them to the table. The Daimler man didn't look as though he had the energy left to make a run for it, but I unholstered my Luger as an additional discouragement.

He shuddered when I tore back the heavily taped seal. A fine, white powder spilled out onto the table. I was pretty certain what it was, but I wanted to be sure. I moistened the tip of my finger and picked up a minute quantity.

The taste was unmistakable. Heroin, smack, horse, or snow. Whatever you called it the end result was the same dark, twisted agony of addiction. I'd seen too many wasted and strung-out kids to feel anything but anger. There was frustration, too, because no matter how hard the drug enforcement people cracked down, it just seemed to keep hitting the streets in even greater amounts.

Well, this was *one* shipment that wasn't going to make it to the market place.

The cottage was modern enough to have indoor plumbing. With Wilhelmina in one hand and the smack tucked under my arm, I herded Daimler into the tiny bathroom.

"Lift up the seat," I snarled.

"No," he screamed, "you can't . . ."

I cut off his babbling by raking his spine with Wilhelmina's barrel. "Now do it," I commanded him.

With trembling hands he lifted the toilet seat. "We can make a deal," he said urgently, "if only *monsieur* would listen to reason."

His whining was starting to get on my nerves. I held the open bag over the bowl and watched it empty into the rust-colored water. I tore open the second bag and repeated the process. I glanced at Daimler and saw tears welling up in the corners of his eyes. A real sentimental bastard was my diplomatic friend.

"Bon voyage," I said softly. I yanked the chain on the overhead tank and smiled as nearly half a million in heroin was sucked into the French sewer system.

"Let's go," I prodded Daimler. "There's one more thing we've got to take care of."

I think he sensed what I was going to do next. In spite of the Luger, he began to claw at my sleeve. I whirled around and clipped him on the jaw. The blow sent him staggering into the middle of the room where his legs folded under him. He hit the floor with a thud, a thin trickle of blood snaking down from his gaping mouth.

"I know it isn't the right season for it," I said cheerfully, "but a good fire always makes things so much cozier."

I picked up the attaché case and carried it over to the empty grate. I thumbed back the clasps and the thick bundles of bills came tumbling out. Looking back at Daimler I saw that his face was a frozen mask of horror.

"It's not *mine,*" he screamed with sudden animation. "They'll kill me if I lose that money."

I smiled and scraped a match across the brickwork. "Too bad," I said softly. "You should have thought about that before you got yourself involved in this little stint. I know you didn't waste any time thinking about all the lives it would ruin."

I dropped the match into the grate.

"You'd better get going," I said, tossing him the empty briefcase. "Because you have to run now and you're never going to be able to stop. We both know they'll find you eventually. It's only a matter of time."

I don't know how much of it he heard. His eyes were locked into a hypnotic stare, the object of which was the pile of burning money.

I turned back and glanced at it myself. The bills crinkled and blackened in the dancing flames. In another minute or so there would be nothing left but a small pile of smoldering ash.

"Move it," I bellowed.

That shook him out of his trance. He pulled himself up from the floor and shuffled over to the door. With his hand on the knob, he turned and said in a pleading voice, "Can I have my gun back, *monsieur?*"

I'd almost forgotten about the Walther I'd taken away from him. I knew he didn't have the nerve to try and use it on me. Maybe he wasn't going to run, but take the quick way out instead. I slid the little PPK out of my belt and tossed it over to him. Whatever he wanted it for, it wasn't my concern anymore.

I had other things in mind. Since this obviously was a dope deal and not an assassination attempt, I still had my embassy killer to track down.

I watched the Daimler man slip out the door and heard the sound of his car driving off a minute later. At least I'd learned one thing tonight—it *always* pays to trust your instincts. Despite all the evidence to the contrary, I'd always felt Gail wasn't the assassin I was looking for. Now I knew the reason why.

"You really whipped him through the hoops," Gail whispered as I crouched down beside her. The wound in her shoulder had stopped bleeding, but her eyes had a faraway, glassy look to them. She wasn't dying. She was just doped up halfway to dreamland.

"Where are your track marks?" I asked curtly.

She looked up at me and sighed. "Under the silver armband I always wear. That's why I didn't take it off when we made love yesterday. I didn't want you to see them, Nick."

"You can't hide them all the time," I said quietly. "What do you do when you're on a modeling job?"

"Cover them up with make-up," she answered softly. Her hand reached out and her long, tapered fingers wrapped themselves around my wrist. "I didn't mean to shoot at you, Nick. I didn't even *know* it was you until after I'd fired. It's lucky my aim isn't too good anymore."

"How the hell did you get into this mess?" I demanded gruffly.

"Through Rodrigo. He got me hooked on amphetamines first. I'm not saying I wasn't willing; I needed them at the time to keep my weight down. He'd just give me another handful whenever I started to crash. Then he got me 'chipping' smack and it wasn't long before I needed to shoot up twice a day or I'd be climbing the walls. *That's* when I found out he wasn't giving it away."

"What did you have to do in return?" I asked gently.

She looked up at me and tried to smile. "Sleep with some diplomats Rodrigo wanted to get a handle on. He had a camera rigged in my bedroom. When some of the older married men got a look at the pictures they were more than willing to do anything he asked. Of course, as diplomats they didn't have to open their bags for customs inspection and he used them to smuggle heroin and money too."

"What about the guy who was here tonight?"

Gail let out a soft, breathy laugh. "Kimmler," she said contemptuously. "Nobody had to blackmail him into it. He *came* to Rodrigo looking to get in on the action."

I was relieved to hear it. The man I'd called "Daimler" hadn't acted like an innocent victim of blackmail and I was glad I hadn't treated him like one.

"Later," Gail continued in a weary voice, "Rodrigo told me I would have to front for the operation, too. Handle all the pickups and deliveries on my own while he and his right-hand man, Hector, watched from a safe distance in case there was trouble. He even had my guns shipped over here so I could carry them on the job. I hadn't touched them since my father died," she added in a whisper.

I reached down and picked her up, moving my arm so that her head rested comfortably on my shoulder.

"You going to carry me off on your snow-white charger?" she asked me softly. "Nick the knight errant, slayer of Hispanic dragons, rescuer of doper damsels in distress.''

"I'm taking you to the American Hospital in Neuilly," I informed her. "I have a doctor friend there who can help you kick the habit and go straight, so you can start living your life like a *human being* again. It won't be easy and it'll take a long time. But you're not so far gone that you couldn't do it if you *wanted* to."

"I do want to," she whispered. "I wanted to tell you about it yesterday afternoon. Don't ask me why; I guess you just looked like someone I could trust. That's why I called you back as you were leaving. Then when I saw you again, I just couldn't get the words out."

"I understand," I said gently.

I carried her along the deserted road, the breeze blowing her soft, fragrant hair in my face. When we reached the Ferrari I tucked her in the passenger seat and drove back to the cottage to collect all the hardware.

All the things that had puzzled me about Gail fell into place—the radical mood-swings, the guns, the tricked-out bedroom. Even the overflowing ashtrays were clear to me now: the compulsive smoking of an addict sweating it out until her next fix. If she had the kind of guts I thought she did, there never would be a "next" fix.

I sensed she was telling the truth about how Rodrigo had victimized her. If the *flics* found out about her part in the operation, I would use what influence I could to keep her out of prison.

It was nearly nine before I dropped Gail off in

the hospital parking lot. I would have liked to have taken her in myself, but I couldn't exactly hang around to explain the gun wound to the cops.

Instead, I phoned my doctor friend and watched from the shadows on the opposite side of Boulevard Victor Hugo as a pair of attendants carried her in on a stretcher. She was in safe hands now.

This morning I'd watched a terrorist group die in an explosion and this evening I'd busted a dope ring.

Now all I had left to do was find an assassin and enough missing weapons to start a war.

Chapter Seventeen

Like a replay of the previous night, there was once again a message waiting for me at the concierge's desk.

At least there was nothing mysterious about this one. It was written in the neat, sloping handwriting I knew almost as well as my own. "If you should return before eleven," it read, "then meet me at the Café Renard Rouge." There was no signature, just a bold letter "H." That was the way my boss, David Hawk, always signed notes and memos.

I had plenty of time so I decided to stop off at my room first. Earlier that evening I'd noticed that the stitching on my shoulder holster was beginning to come loose. It was a minor thing really, but sometimes your survival can depend on something as insignificant as a couple of worn-out threads. I didn't have another shoulder rig in my luggage, but I did have an ankle holster I occasionally used when I wanted to carry a second handgun. It would have to do until I got the other one repaired.

When I entered my room, I knew almost immediately that Lauren was gone. There was a stillness about the place, an emptiness that made it suddenly seem like just another lonely hotel room.

It was turning out to be my night for notes. I found Lauren's pinned to the pillow: "Dearest Nick," it began, "I have returned to my apartment. When you have finished whatever it is you came to Paris to do, you'll find me waiting there for you. Take care of yourself and don't keep me waiting too long. Love, Lauren."

I was partly relieved and partly disappointed that she had finally taken my advice. I folded the sheet of cream-colored hotel stationery and tucked it into my jacket pocket. At least I knew where she was and that she'd have round-the-clock protection until this terrorist thing was finally resolved.

I slipped out of my jacket and unbuckled my shoulder holster. From the look of the seam where the two straps crossed over, it was bound to give way after a couple more wearings. I found the ankle job at the bottom of my suitcase and strapped it around my right leg. I had to readjust the velcro fittings a couple of times before it felt comfortable. After reloading Wilhelmina, I tucked her away in her new home. I wasn't entirely satisfied, but it would just have to do for the time being.

I'd already parked the car in the garage for the night, so I decided to walk the short distance to Boissier's café. Considering what I'd been through that day, I felt surprisingly fit. I knew a lot of it was due to the adrenalin I had worked up during all the action at the cottage. For the moment it was overriding all my "invalid" pains, but as soon as it stopped flowing, the aching and throbbing would start up again.

Paris always has been one of my favorite cities for walking. Tonight I just strolled along like a tourist taking in all the sights. The sidewalk cafés were crowded with couples of all ages, heads close together under brightly colored umbrellas while overhead neon signs spelled out their messages in glowing, vibrant shades. I passed old crones hawking the *Loterie Nationale,* their voices a shrill counterpoint to the sounds from the cafés. Every few blocks the shadowed doorways housed a prostitute. Young or old, they beckoned me with the same wary eyes and the kind of smile that hadn't changed since the Stone Age.

I crossed to the Left Bank via the Pont des Invalides, one of the thirty-two bridges that span the Seine as it flows through Paris. Another ten minutes of walking brought me to the doorstep of the Café Renard Rouge.

As usual, Boissier was packing them in. The mix of people here was a little bit different, though, from the standard Parisian café. There were students, of course, and artists who wore their paint and clay-stained jeans like some kind of badge of office. But right along with them there was a sizable percentage of petty criminals. They were difficult to spot—the rumpled but flashy clothes, the low-voiced conversation, the way their eyes flicked over the room every few seconds as if they were anxiously waiting for an overdue friend.

A thick blue haze of cigarette smoke hung over the tables like a cloud. In the far corner a gaudy-looking juke box blared out the latest French version of an old American rock tune. Boissier wasn't behind the bar. The man who was, turned away from the espresso machine just long enough to point me in the right direction.

I found my boss and the burly Frenchman in a booth at the back, a nearly empty carafe of calvados centered on the table between them.

"Nick," Boissier's booming voice greeted me. "Now our evening is complete. Sit down and let me have a look at you. David here says you've collected a few cuts and scrapes since I saw you this morning."

I slipped in next to Hawk and grinned at Boissier as he slowly assessed the damage with his bloodshot eyes. "You'll live," he pronounced finally, "but not without a shot of calvados. Jean," he bellowed, "another glass and a fresh carafe, too. We have some serious drinking to do here."

A harried waiter appeared with both items in something like thirty seconds. I'd always known there were advantages to owning your own bar.

"How was your trip?" Hawk asked me quietly.

"Interesting," I replied after a moment's hesitation. "Not exactly what I'd expected, but interesting just the same."

He nodded silent understanding and turned back to our host. That was all either one of us could say in front of a third party. Even though Boissier was one of my boss's oldest friends, it would be a flagrant violation of AXE regulations to talk about an assignment in his presence. Hawk's question had merely been a way of checking to see if I had anything I urgently needed to tell him.

As for Boissier knowing about my "accident," that was only logical. First, it was Boissier's tip that had sent me to Vitry and second, the news of the explosion had been in all the evening papers. It was only natural that he ask Hawk if I'd been injured. And since the state of my health was hardly top secret, Hawk had answered him truthfully.

"Drink up," Boissier prompted, "I've got another eight barrels of this stuff in the cellar. You're lucky you didn't get here any earlier, Nick," he said, turning to me with a wolfish grin. "You would have had to sit around and look respectfully bored while two old windbags told lies to each other about how they ran the Germans out of France single-handed. Isn't that right, David, *mon ami.*"

"Yes, André." There was a certain wistfulness in the simple answer that I had never heard in Hawk's voice before. It went along with the way they said each other's names, *first* names, a rarity with Hawk; and the surprisingly calm expression on Hawk's normally aggressive features.

I knew exactly what it was. The look of an old man remembering his youth.

"It was simpler back then," Hawk said reflectively. "Everything seemed so clear-cut, so black-and-white. You knew who your enemies and allies were and you knew the job that had to be done. It isn't that way anymore," he said, pausing to blow a spiral of smoke toward the ceiling. "It's more gray than anything else and alliances change faster than the weather. Sometimes I really miss those years," Hawk added quietly.

"So do I," Boissier said chuckling, "but I think we both have *very* selective memories. The good times we recall, but not the bad."

After that the conversation took a less philosophical turn and I listened as the two of them swapped stories about some of the craziest things that had happened to them during the war. There's one about Hawk, three French girls, and a tank that he'd already made me swear an oath not to repeat.

We left the café around eleven and headed back to the hotel at a leisurely pace.

"At least that's one suspect eliminated," Hawk said after I'd given him a report of the evening's events. "It's also my opinion that the group wiped out by this morning's explosion *was* the one responsible for the assassinations and the weapons smuggling. Their race and politics certainly fit the pattern and if there were *another* group like that operating in Paris, I'm sure Boissier would know about it."

"I'm sure you're right," I agreed. "But we still need to find the girl and the missing weapons. Do you think there's less of a threat now as far as the Arab oil conference is concerned?"

"Less," Hawk replied curtly, "but one we certainly can't ignore. We still have to wrap this affair up with all due speed." He paused at the railing of the bridge and tossed his cigar stub into the dark, murky water. "I found out something interesting tonight," he said casually. "That Ann-Marie Michaels is the granddaughter of a woman who used to work with Boissier and me in the Resistance. A very pretty girl as I remember, code name Crescent."

"Maybe you'll get a chance to look her up before you leave Paris," I suggested.

"No," Hawk said quietly. "The Gestapo caught her back in '43."

Chapter Eighteen

When the phone woke me the following morning, I immediately noticed two things. One, the empty place where Lauren had slept on the other side of the bed, and two, how high and bright the sun was in the morning sky.

I looked at my watch on the bedside table. A quarter past eleven. I'd slept a lot later than I'd intended to and my head felt groggy, as though someone had wrapped my brain in a thick layer of cotton wool.

I scooped up the phone on the second ring and grunted hello.

"Nick," a familiar voice greeted me, "this is Jeff Bellows. I'm in Christine Dalton's apartment on Rue le Nôtre. You don't have to rush, but there's something here I think you ought to see."

"Like what?" I demanded. But Bellows, in his usual laconic manner, had already spoken his piece. I was talking into a dead line.

I eased myself out of bed, took a quick shower, and dressed. My head still throbbed and my mouth felt dry, as though I'd been drinking all night instead of just for an hour. I decided it was probably the mixture of Boissier's apple brandy and the injuries I'd sustained from the explosion. Still, it bothered me that my thinking and reflexes weren't nearly as sharp as they should be.

The midmorning traffic was light and I made good time driving to the Rue le Nôtre. It's a tiny, block-long street on the Right Bank of the Seine, just where the river begins to curve southward again. On the opposite bank I could see the Eiffel Tower, its gray metal skeleton rising almost a thousand feet above the Champs de Mars.

Christine Dalton lived in one of those small, ultramodern apartment complexes. You see them all over the world now. Built fast and without too much care. The kind of place where the walls are so thin that you can hear your next-door neighbor's breathing.

I rapped on her door and waited while Bellows scrutinized me through the peephole. A half-second later the bolt slid back and he opened the door just wide enough to let me slip inside.

"Why all the precautions?" I ask him gruffly. "You expecting someone besides me?"

"You'll see," he replied. That's what I liked about Jeff. He never used three words when two would do.

The place was a modest, L-shaped studio. A couch, a couple of director's chairs, and a table—surprisingly spartan for someone who made big money as a top fashion model.

But the real surprise was around the corner where Bellows was leading me. Christine Dalton herself.

She was stretched out on the narrow bed with her eyes closed. I'd seen enough of them to quickly realize that she wasn't ever going to be opening those ice blue eyes again. Not in this world, anyway.

On the night table next to her was an empty barbiturate bottle and a glass. They were standing in front of a photograph in a heavy silver frame. I recognized the ruddy, blond good looks of the man in the picture.

He was one of the terrorists I'd seen blown to bits yesterday morning in Vitry.

My eyes moved back to the peaceful-looking figure on the bed. She was dressed in a quilted blue robe; no make-up, jewelry, or other extras. There was a slight half-smile on her lips. Of all the people I'd seen die since I'd come to Paris, she was the only one who looked as though she might have enjoyed it.

"Any signs of a struggle?" I asked abruptly.

Bellows sighed and shook his head. "I checked out the body before I phoned you. Everything coincides with the obvious conclusion, Nick. Suicide."

"This is all very convenient," I said skeptically. "Maybe a little too convenient. That picture by the bed is a photograph of one of the terrorists I saw die yesterday. It makes for a very pat scenario, a real soap opera episode. Grief stricken over her lover's death, beautiful assassin takes her own life. I can practically see the headline in the *Midnight Globe*. But I *still* don't buy it," I snapped.

"That's because you haven't seen everything yet," he answered with a complacent smile. He took his pipe out of his mouth and pointed the chewed-up stem toward the floor. "Lift up those boards in the corner," he suggested.

As I bent down I saw that they were already loose. Four long pine planks, each one about six inches wide. I pried up the nearest one and found myself looking at the launching component of a Redeye missile.

"Well, well," I said softly. "This does cast things in a different light."

"I thought you'd say that," Bellows replied smugly. "Along with the missile, I've so far unearthed two dozen M-16s, nightscopes, grenades, and a lot of very sophisticated communications equipment. Unless I'm mistaken," he added, "all those items were on a list of smuggled arms that we've been trying to trace."

"You're right," I informed him, "but there's one thing you haven't told me. What are you doing here *in* the apartment?"

Bellows shrugged and gave me a foolish grin. "I know I was just supposed to stake the place out," he said quickly, "but I started getting worried when I hadn't seen the girl in over sixteen hours. I guess I was afraid she'd given me the slip," he admitted quietly. His pudgy features had taken on the expression of a ten-year-old caught with his hand in the cookie jar.

"So you decided to check it out," I prompted.

"I know it was against orders," he said, turning away from my stern-eyed gaze. "When I got here I found the door unlocked, a common trait of suicides, particularly women who want their bodies discovered before the decaying process sets in. I saw the body and called you right away. I decided to do a little poking around while I was waiting for you to arrive and that's how I uncovered the weapons cache."

"I don't know whether to reprimand you or thank you," I said evenly. "Probably the latter, since this seems to tie up all the loose ends. I questioned the suicide at first; we all know how easy it is to fake something like that. But even if people were able to slip in and out without you seeing them, there's no way they could have planted all this hardware here overnight."

Bellows nodded silent agreement. "What do you want me to do now, Nick?"

"Sit tight," I told him. "I'd like to have some of our lab people go over this just to make sure we haven't missed anything. When they're finished," I added, smiling, "you can call the police from a pay phone with an anonymous tip about a dead body."

When I left the apartment, I knew I had a call of my own to make. I stopped in a little *bar tabac* and got a *jeton* for the phone from the man behind the counter.

"You just caught me on my way out," Hawk's crisp voice stated after we had exchanged hellos.

"I'm glad I did, sir. I've got some news I think you'll be very happy to hear."

He listened patiently to my report of the morning's events. When I finished there was a brief pause. I heard him strike a match and draw a deep breath. He was lighting up another one of his "El Defectos." I could almost smell the foul odor over the phone line.

"I'm satisfied," he said finally. "As you know, the oil summit starts today. I spoke to their security people an hour ago and they've got the place sealed up as tight as a mummy's tomb. If what they say is true, it would be impossible to get any kind of weapon in there without it being detected."

"Is there anything you'd like me to do?" I asked.

"Yes," he said gruffly. "Take a couple of days off and rest. And don't think I'm going soft," he added, chuckling, "I just want you fit enough to be in East Berlin on Thursday."

Before I could ask him why, he hung up the phone.

Chapter Nineteen

My first act of freedom was to stop at a café for an overdue breakfast of coffee and croissants. Filling my stomach seemed to help my headache, too; by the time I'd finished my second café au lait it had diminished to a dull, but not very painful throbbing.

I lit a cigarette, tipped back my chair, and began debating what I should do with my two days of leave. Naturally, all my plans included Lauren. It would be interesting, not to mention pleasant, to see how we got on without anyone shooting at us or chasing us. I had a feeling we'd both enjoy the change.

We could leave town and stay at a country inn. There was a wonderful one, the Hôtel d' Angleterre, in Chantilly. I hadn't been there in years, but I could still remember the taste of the chef's specialty, turbot in bérnaise sauce. Even closer to Paris there was Longchamps, the world-famous racetrack, or we could spend a day on one of those double-decked tourist boats that cruise up and down the Seine. Whatever we decided on, I'd make sure we left ample time for *l'amour*.

I tossed a bill down on the marble-topped table and headed for the car. I still had a few minor things to take care of back at the hotel. After that, I'd phone Lauren and we could get my two days of "R and R" underway with lunch at Maxim's.

As I eased the Ferrari into the traffic flow, I couldn't help feeling a certain dissatisfaction with the way this assignment had resolved itself. Of course, I was glad it was over. No question about that. I guess what really bothered me was how little I'd contributed to the successful completion.

All through the case I'd been a step or two *behind* my quarry. Kind of like a long-distance race where you never quite manage to catch up with the lead runner. I located the terrorist group and before I could question them they all die in an explosion. While I'm closing in on Gail Huntington and the drug ring, the *real* assassin is committing suicide. And part of the missing weapons cache is found under her floor, tying all three incidents together into a neat little package.

Where was I all that time? Getting shot at, chased, attacked with knives, or blasted through the air. Not exactly fun, but nothing I hadn't been through countless times before. The problem was I should have been able to handle all of that and *still* uncovered the terrorists and Christine Dalton.

Maybe it was just the way these things work out sometimes. Coincidences, timing, matters beyond my control. Or possibly there was a simpler an-

swer. One that I didn't want to admit even to myself.

I was getting too old for the game.

Why not? It happens to everyone sooner or later.
I wasn't any more timeless or indestructable than
the next man down the line. Perhaps a year from
now I'd be using a desk and telephone instead of
Hugo, Wilhelmina, and Pierre. No more Killmaster status. N3 retired for good.

I parked the car in the garage and went up to my
room. During the short elevator ride, I managed to
quell some of the frustration I was feeling. I even
was able to half convince myself that I was just
having a bad day. Finally I, decided to shelve this
kind of thinking until after I'd finished my leave.
There was no point in spoiling my two days with
Lauren. I could never be sure when I'd see her or
Paris again.

I turned the key in the lock and opened the door.

The three men stood in a half-circle, the muzzles
of their M-16's all pointing at the same target—me.

For a moment we were motionless, silent. They
knew I was considering all my options and discard-
ing them just as quickly. They also knew that there
was nothing I could do that wouldn't get me killed.
Instantly.

"Bon jour," I said impishly. "If there's some
problem about the hotel bill, I'm sure we can work
it . . ."

"Cut the crap," the one in the center commanded in French. He was in his early fifties and
had a weathered, sun-blackened face and a distinct

military bearing. If I only had one guess, I would have said he was a veteran of the Algerian conflict.

The two men flanking him were younger, but cut from the same mold. Hard, competent professionals. Their cold, narrow eyes said they'd done this kind of thing many times before.

"Now, Monsieur Carter, reach out very slowly and pull the door shut behind you."

I followed the older man's instructions. When I finished, he smiled at me as if I were some three-year-old who'd finally learned how to tie his shoelaces.

"That's good," he said with a soft chuckle. "Next, I'd like you to lace your fingers together behind your head."

Why not, I decided. Maybe I'd get another yellow-toothed smile.

When I assumed the position, the man on the left put down his M-16 and began to disarm me. He took Hugo first, then he dropped to his knees and slipped my Luger out of the ankle holster. He hadn't even bothered to pat down my torso for a shoulder rig. He *knew* where I kept my gun.

"All right," the old man said. "Now that that's finished, there's someone in the next room who wants to talk to you, Carter."

I nodded wordlessly. They didn't have to tell me who it was. I already knew who was waiting on the other side of the door.

Chapter Twenty

"Nick, *mon ami*. You don't look very surprised to see me?"

"I'm not," I replied evenly. "One of your men did something that gave you away. A minor mistake, but sloppy tradecraft just the same."

"And what was that?" he demanded. His red-rimmed eyes were intense with anger.

"The ankle holster," I said coolly. "Your boy went straight for it; he had been told where I kept my gun. Since I only switched it from my usual carrying place last night, it *had* to be you. You're sharp enough to have noticed the change and you're the only person outside the organization I've seen since I made it."

André Boissier tossed back his head and laughed. There was an odd, maniacal edge to the sound that reminded me of the laughter I'd once heard while visiting a lunatic asylum outside Buenos Aires. Not that I thought Boissier was ready for one. My guess was that he was long overdue.

When it had died down to a soft chuckle he said,

"That's very astute of you, Nick. But I'm afraid the revelation came a little too late to be of any help to you. Or to David Hawk."

"Hawk?" I repeated. My throat was suddenly dry and tight. I swallowed hard, trying to get the words out. "Is he dead?" I asked in a broken whisper.

"Not yet," Boissier answered. "I figure he'll last two weeks, maybe three. I sold him to the Chinese," he explained with a wolfish grin. "One slightly used senior intelligence officer in exchange for a large shipment of assorted weapons. Not a bad deal," he added lightly. "But I know the Chinese will want to get full value out of my old comrade in arms. They have a way of getting information out of a man . . . well, I won't bore you with the details. Let's just say there isn't much left when they're finished."

"You son of a bitch," I muttered through clenched teeth. "Where is he now? On his way to China?"

Boissier shrugged. "I suppose there's no reason for me not to tell you. Because we both know there isn't the faintest chance of your leaving this room alive."

I'd been waiting for him to say it. Not that it wasn't something I hadn't already figured out for myself.

The burly Frenchman was seated twenty feet away from me on the opposite side of the room. And like his three friends, he was toting an M-16. If I tried to rush him, I'd be dead before I got halfway there. I also knew that someone with his experience wouldn't let me edge my way any closer. I'd lost my Luger and stiletto, and in a situation like this, Pierre, my tiny gas bomb, was useless. Without some kind of weapon I was as good as dead already.

"No, Hawk isn't in transit yet," Boissier continued. "The Chinese are going to pick him up at an abandoned air strip outside Vernon in a little more than an hour from now."

"Why?" I asked quietly. I asked partly to stall for time, but I really *did* want to know why we'd both been betrayed by one of my boss's oldest and closest friends.

"For France," the old man bellowed. "For the new order and glory our revolution will bring to it. Too long my country has been wallowing in the mire of bureaucracy, held back by cowardly liberals and compromising weaklings. We've been stripped of our rightful colonies and what have we gotten in return? A flood of racially inferior scum who take jobs away from honest Frenchmen because they're willing to work for a few francs a day. Under the new order," he said fanatically, "all of that will come to an end."

This is just an old lunatic raving, I told myself. Even with the weapons and manpower, nothing like that could actually happen. Then I suddenly remembered where I'd heard Boissier's words before. From films and recordings of a former house painter who rose to world power. A man who had conquered France himself once. A man whom both

Boissier and Hawk had fought against in their younger days.

If it could happen once, it could happen again.

"You'll never pull it off," I told him.

"Yes I will," he answered fervently. "I have arms cached all over the country, enough arms to start a revolution and enough men to carry them. In half an hour a massive explosion will wipe out the entire delegation to the Arab oil summit. All attention will be focused on that, on Paris. The army and national guard will be mobilized, sent in to help handle the situation. While they're looking in the other direction, my men will rise up and take over key military installations and communications centers all over the rest of France. It's a simple but effective ploy," he added, smiling. "I used it numerous times on a smaller scale during the Resistance."

"You'll never get a bomb anywhere near the oil conference," I said smugly. "Their security is virtually impenetrable."

All this got me was another burst of insane laughter. *"Now* it is impenetrable," he said when the spasm had subsided, "but a year ago there was no security at all. You see, *mon ami,* I've been planning this day for a long time. During the last fifteen months we've planted huge charges of *plastique* in a dozen major hotels and government buildings all over Paris. The bomb at the Georges V, where the Arabs are meeting, has been there for more than a year now, patiently waiting for the day I would have a use for it. Ingenious, no?"

In spite of myself, I nodded wordless agreement.

"The rest of the charges," he continued, "will be triggered later today. Then Paris will be in such turmoil that no one will even be aware that we've taken over the rest of the country." He paused and reached down for something beside his chair. I was tempted to make a try for him, but his other hand kept the M-16 trained steadily on target.

"A drink to victory," he said, hoisting a bottle of calvados. He tilted it back and took a long pull, a tiny rivulet of liquor running down his grizzled beard. "To victory," he muttered again, wiping his mouth with the back of his sleeve. He wedged the bottle between his legs and stuck the cork back in. "Finish it off," he said, tossing it on the bed. "I've got to keep a clear head. And don't try throwing it at me," he cautioned. "You'll be dead before it ever leaves your hand."

The warning was hardly necessary. A bottle of apple brandy wouldn't be of any use to me, not against an M-16. Or would it? The plan that was forming in my head was almost as crazy as Boissier's plot to overthrow the government.

But I had to try it.

"Thanks," I said smiling. I perched on the edge of the bed, uncorked the bottle, and drank. The fiery warmth of the brandy flooded my body and eased some of the tension that had been building steadily since I entered the room. I pushed the cork back in and put the bottle down beside me. "Mind if I have a cigarette?" I asked casually. "Last wish of a condemned man and all that."

"Go ahead," Boissier replied, grinning. "But any fast moves and I squeeze the trigger."

I nodded compliance and slowly eased out my cigarette case and lighter. Along with them I pulled out the folded white handkerchief I always carry. Slowly I used it to wipe the sweat from my face. I tossed it down on the bed and lit a cigarette with equal slowness. "You were behind everything," I said with a hint of admiration in my voice. "I should have realized it from the beginning."

"But of course, *mon ami*," said Boissier. "All the assassinations, the explosion at Vitry (in which I intended you to die by the way), Christine's supposed suicide. They were all the work of my people."

"I'm sure you're telling the truth," I said, "but there are a couple of things that I can't figure out. First, why kill diplomats from other countries when you intend to take over *France?* And second, if Christine wasn't an assassin working for you, then how did you manage to plant that cache of weapons while my people had the building under surveillance? A Redeye missle isn't exactly something you can carry in under your coat," I added wryly.

He beamed at me like a teacher about to explain a simple equation to a particularly slow student. "The assassinations served a dual purpose," he began. "Primarily they were done to cause a state of unrest in the country, but also to focus the intelligence community's attention on the killings rather than on my *real* work, the smuggling and distribution of arms on a massive scale. If it hadn't been for that accident at the airport," he flared, "none of you would ever have caught on."

"And the arms in the girl's apartment?"

"They'd been there for months," he said, chuckling. "Christine and Ann-Marie were close friends, so Ann-Marie had no trouble getting hold of the Dalton girl's keys long enough to duplicate them. When she was out of town one weekend, we smuggled them in and hid them under the floor boards. I don't think she ever realized they were there. It made for a convenient depository close at hand and when we needed a dead assassin . . . well, the setup was too good not to use."

"There's only one woman left," I said softly. "Ann-Marie."

"Who else?" said Boissier shrugging. "While Gail was busy making herself *look* like the assassin, a bit of luck I had no part in, Ann-Marie quietly and skillfully terminated all the necessary people. Such a cheerful, considerate girl on the surface, the last person you would imagine to be a professional assassin."

"Is she handling the oil summit, too?" I asked softly.

"No one else, *mon ami*. She's in the press room on the floor below the conference. Ann-Marie is impersonating a journalist and part of her equipment is naturally a tape recorder. Built into that recorder is a small, short-range transmitter that will trigger the bomb." Boissier looked at the clock on the night table and smiled. "The Georges V is only a few blocks away. We should hear the blast in about fifteen minutes."

I had to move fast now. I didn't have much of a chance, but I had to try it. Nothing else stood between Boissier and the bloodbath he was about to unleash on an unsuspecting France.

"You think there's a place in your organization for me?" I asked eagerly. If I could only keep him talking for another minute or so, I might pull it off.

"No," he answered regretfully, "I really don't think so. You're a good man, Carter, but I'd never be able to completely trust you. For the good of the cause, you'll have to be eliminated."

I gave him what I hoped was a look of resignation and took a long pull from the bottle of calvados. I put it down and wiped my mouth with the handkerchief, spitting out the unswallowed brandy as the cloth passed over my lips. I put the sodden handkerchief on the bed and muttered a silent prayer that Boissier hadn't caught on to what I was trying to do.

"A final cigarette?" I asked in a voice that cracked with tension. If he denied the request I'd never get out of this room alive.

He stared at me for a moment as if he were trying to come to a decision. I took a deep breath and fought to keep my pounding heart under control.

"One," he snapped. "After that we must say au revoir."

I picked up my case slowly, took out one of my custom-made cigarettes, and put it in my mouth.

My left hand was wrapped around the neck of the brandy bottle. With my right I scooped up the lighter and handkerchief.

It was now or never. I jumped behind the bed.

Boissier had expected me to come *at* him, not hide. The small edge of surprise allowed me to take cover before the M-16 stitched the wall behind me with a burst of rapid fire.

Working at top speed, I centered the cork on the calvados-soaked handkerchief and slammed it back into the bottle. I thumbed my lighter into flame and touched it to the cloth. It erupted into a twisting blue-gold flame.

Bullets pounded into the bed now. In another second Boissier would cut me down with the M-16.

I leaned back and heaved the bottle as hard as I could.

The explosion sounded tremendous in the confines of the room. I heard the sound of shattering glass, then a horrible high-pitched scream. A heartbeat later the M-16 hit the floor with a hard, metallic thump.

I looked up and saw Boissier dancing wildly around the room, his head, torso, and arms enveloped in a sheet of flame. The Molotov cocktail I'd thrown blind must have hit its target directly.

Trying vainly to put out the blaze, he staggered onto the balcony. He no longer looked like a man, but a charred mass of burning flesh instead. His mouth was open wide in a single, constant scream of agony.

Boissier hit the balcony railing and toppled over

it. The scream diminished as he plunged to the street and struck the pavement with a sickening thud. I watched as a group of gape-mouthed passersby gathered around the motionless form.

Now that Boissier was dead, I had no more time to waste on him. I'd picked up the M-16, expecting his three henchmen to come pouring into the room with guns blazing. But they must have taken off after turning me over to their leader because when I eased open the door to the adjoining room, it was empty.

I hastily collected Hugo and Wilhelmina, and then ran down the corridor toward the lobby stairs. I only had a few minutes to get to the Georges V and stop Ann-Marie.

Another bit of knowledge wrenched at my gut like a gnawing animal. Whether I stopped the girl or not, I'd still be too late to save Hawk.

Chapter Twenty-One

I screeched to a halt in front of the canopied entrance and leapt out of the Farrari.

"Leave it here," I snapped at the startled attendant. "Keep the motor running and don't let anyone touch it."

Before he could frame a reply, I pressed a hundred franc note in his hand and bounded through the ornate double doors. I got about three feet before a half-dozen men in khaki uniforms formed a tight circle around me. They were members of the CRS, the *Compagnie Républicaine de Sécurité,* France's elite paramilitary police.

"Where do you think you're going?" the one with the officer's stripes demanded.

I grinned sheepishly. "Sorry about barging in like that, but I'm late for the conference. If you'll just direct me to the press desk, I'll check in properly."

He stared at me for a second, then held out his hand. "Your identification, Monsieur."

I sighed and handed him my wallet. He studied

the Amalgamated Press card and then compared the photograph on it to my face. Precious seconds ticked by while he scrutinized my features.

I toyed with the idea of telling him why I was here. But I knew he probably wouldn't believe me and if he *did* we'd have to go through the proper *channels* before any action was taken. By then it would be too late.

"The press desk is at the rear of the lobby," he said, handing me back my wallet. "Two of my men will accompany you there and after you've checked in, escort you to the press room."

I muttered a quick "merci" and slipped out of the circle. Two of the heavily armed CRS *flics* took up positions on either side of me. Hawk had been right when he said security was tight.

I waited impatiently while a man at the desk gave my press card a second close inspection. Finally, he filled out a plastic pin-on badge with my name and handed it to me. With my two guards flanking me, I headed for the elevator.

I looked at my watch. If Boissier hadn't been lying, I had two minutes left to stop the girl.

My heart almost stopped instead when I saw the familiar frame of a metal detector. There were ten CRS's grouped around it, all toting MAS-52 machine guns. I knew there was no way I could make it through without their discovering my Luger and stiletto. If I tried to make a run for it I'd never reach the elevator alive.

"Hang on a second," I muttered in French. "I

think I left my wallet back at the desk."

"*Allons,*" the guard on my right snapped. *Allons,* roughly translated, means keep moving. In case I'd missed his meaning, he prodded me with his truncheon in the direction of the metal detector.

That was it. I was finished.

As I neared the heavily guarded frame, I heard a voice calling my name. I spun on my heel as General Clarke Willoby slapped his hand on my shoulder.

"Damn, Carter, it *is* you," he bellowed. "I thought these tired old eyes were playing tricks on me. Let's get out of this dump and get ourselves a drink."

"I'm trying to get *in,*" I said quickly. "And I've got to get through that metal detector without being stopped. It's a national security matter," I added hastily.

"Say no more, son," he said, slipping his arm around my shoulder. My two watchdogs had already melted back into the crowd. We walked through the metal detector together, setting off a wild clammering of bells.

A CRS man stepped in our path, his machine gun at port arms. Willoby looked at the man with cold, steel-hard eyes. The *flic's* glance dropped away taking in the "spinach," the NATO insignia and the stars on the General's shoulders. He quickly saluted and stepped aside. Who says rank doesn't have its privileges?

We rushed through the open elevator doors and

I jammed the button for the seventh floor, where the press room was. I had less than a minute to stop Ann-Marie.

"I don't know what the hell's going on," the general said, "but you can count on me, Carter. I'm not the kind of man who forgets. Not ever."

What the general was referring to was an incident that had taken place in Bogota some eight years ago. A KGB hit team had been sent in to "terminate him with extreme prejudice." I'd saved Clarke Willoby from that as well as from a plot to discredit him and end his military career. Obviously, he still felt he owed me one. Luckily, he was here at the perfect time for me to collect.

After what seemed a lifetime, the doors opened on a crowded press room. Most of the reporters were staring upward, their eyes glued to the closed-circuit TV monitors that broadcast the action from the floor above, along with a printout that ran along the bottom of the screen translating the Arabic into French and English.

My eyes urgently scanned the room and stopped on a blonde-haired woman. She was one of the few people who wasn't looking up at the monitors. Even though the hair coloring and thick glasses didn't match, her general build was very much like Ann-Marie's. More importantly, she was holding a tape recorder in her hands.

"Ann-Marie," I shouted.

Her head snapped around and she saw me. Her eyes went wide with recognition as she began to frantically push the buttons on the recorder.

I brought Wilhelmina out and aimed just as she dove back into the crowd. Someone screamed as she pushed people out of the way. She was heading for a CRS man, but not for protection.

When she reached him she grabbed the gun from his holster. He tried to collar her, but she darted out of the way. People started hitting the deck as she swung the heavy automatic in my direction.

I squeezed the trigger.

The bullet hit her in the face, plowing a path of spattered blood and bone through her beautiful features. The gun fell from her grasp as her body jackknifed and crashed to the floor.

The impact had knocked her wig askew, freeing a tangle of rich, dark curls. The tape recorder lay at her feet. As the reporters began to crowd around her, I pushed them aside.

"Listen, Willoby," I said urgently, "because I only have time to explain this once."

Chapter Twenty-Two

As I reached the outskirts of Paris, the traffic began to move a little faster. For ten frustrating minutes I'd been trapped in a congested tangle of trucks and cars. Leaning on the horn did no good; something up ahead of us was causing a massive tie-up. My hands drummed a nervous tattoo on the steering wheel. I smoked a cigarette and lit another one from the glowing butt.

Finally, the long line started moving again.

When I cleared the entrance ramp I swung the Ferrari onto the shoulder of the road and stomped on the gas. As advertized the 512 Boxer went from zero to seventy in less than seven seconds. I fought to keep the wheel under control as I sped along the sloping embankment. Spraying a backwash of gravel in my wake, I passed a long line of vehicles that became little more than a multicolored blur.

I saw an opening up ahead and piloted the Ferrari back onto the blacktop. Shifting gears, I pushed the speed up to ninety.

I knew I was racing against time and losing. I

had about fifteen minutes left in which to cover the forty miles to Vernon. At top speed the Boxer 512 *could* do up to one hundred and sixty-four mph. I had taken her up to the max only once before, on a track outside of Florence. But those had been optimum conditions, not a pot-holed and badly maintained French highway.

I would have to try it. I knew I'd never be able to live with myself if I didn't.

David Hawk. My boss and, in a way, my oldest and closest friend. The one unchanging constant in a shadowy world of violence and mistrust.

I shifted again. The speedometer needle climbed with my acceleration. One hundred and ten . . . twenty . . . forty . . . one hundred and sixty.

The road was like an endless black ribbon now, the landscape a smeared rainbow of colors. The car shook violently as the shocks fought to absorb the jolts from the scarred and pitted blacktop.

At least I had two lanes to work with and an open stretch of highway up ahead. If I was going to get there in time to rescue Hawk, I couldn't even afford to slow down for *anything*.

Before leaving Paris I'd hastily told General Willoby about the bomb in the Georges V, the other bombs Boissier had boasted of, and his plans for an uprising all across France.

The general had listened without interruption and promised me he would alert the CRS, the armed forces, and the police. With his NATO status, he was the one man I knew who had the clout and connections to cut through all the red tape and get the job done before it was too late.

I'd considered asking him to send a chopper out to Vernon. But mobilizing American army troops on French soil could easily turn into an international incident with world-wide repercussions. Also, I knew how Hawk felt about involving military personnel in one of our operations. Clarke Willoby he could accept because of the enormity of the situation and my one-to-one relationship with the man. But a chopper combat squad? As Hawk had told me countless times before, "If AXE can't do it on its own, *no one* can."

But this was something different. His own life was in danger now. In spite of that, I was positive he would want me to handle it on my own.

I spotted a farm truck up ahead of me straddling both lanes. There wasn't enough room to pass on either side. Not at the speed I was going.

I leaned on the horn. But as the Ferrari ate up the distance between us, I realized the driver had no intention of pulling over to let me pass.

Forty feet behind him, I eased up on the gas a fraction and swung onto the shoulder of the road. I passed the truck at one forty-five and swerved back onto the blacktop.

The sound was like a gunshot.

I felt the right rear of the car begin to sink and heard the flapping sound of a rapidly deflating tire. I knew, with sickening certainty, I had a flat.

I downshifted and braked to a gradual stop. Leaping out onto the embankment, I saw I'd been right. The right rear tire was a misshapen wreck.

I pulled out my tools and spare, pried off the hubcap, and started to work. My hands moved quickly; I'd performed this familiar task hundreds of times before.

I kept resisting an almost overpowering impulse to look at my watch. Work on the tire, I told myself. Don't think about Hawk. Just work on the *goddamn tire* and get out of here.

I pushed the Michelin XWX into place and finished the job. I'd wasted three, almost four minutes and I had less than that left to get to the airstrip on time.

I knew I'd never make it, but I had to try.

I jumped back into the car and quickly brought the Ferrari back to top speed. If the pickup from Boissier's men went off ahead of schedule, Hawk might already be airborne by now, on his way to mainland China via a route of short country-to-country hops until they reached a secure base. There a jet would be waiting to take him on the long, final leg of a journey from which there would be no return.

As I reached the outskirts of Vernon, I slowed just enough to scan the passing landscape.

Out of the corner of my eye I saw it. A dilapidated wooden tower rising above a flat stretch of open grassland. That *had* to be the old airfield Boissier had referred to.

I swung the car onto an unpaved access road and floored the accelerator. As I rounded a sharp bend, I caught my first glimpse of the plane.

It was taxiing down the runway, a pale blue

Beechcraft Bonanza building up speed for take-off.

There wasn't any time to consider the options. I could only think of one thing to do. And it could wind up getting us all killed.

I aimed the Ferrari toward the speeding plane and floored the accelerator.

I hit the undercarriage with a deafening crash. The impact sent me hurtling against the dashboard. A big hunk of the fuselage shattered the windshield, showering me with broken glass.

With blood streaming down my face, I pulled myself out of the Ferrari. Shots bit into the ground behind me. I swung around with Wilhelmina in my hand and squeezed off three rounds at a man crouched on the wing.

His eyes widened in shocked surprise as the slugs tore open a gushing red hole in his chest. The gun fell from his hand as he slumped forward, draping himself over the wing.

I looked back and saw that the two men in the cockpit had died when the car struck the plane. If Hawk was still alive in there, then why didn't he come out? I knew it was only a matter of seconds before the whole damn mess went up in flames.

As I raced for the plane, he appeared in the doorway. He was staggering badly, one hand clutching his forehead where a dark trickle of blood oozed between his fingers.

"Hawk!" I screamed.

He looked up just as I grabbed him and tossed his thin body unceremoniously over my shoulder. I ran for my life, for both our lives.

I'd gone about two hundred feet when the car and the plane exploded into a huge ball of searing orange flame.

Chapter Twenty-Three

It turned cold the morning they buried Boissier. The sky overhead was a deep slate blue and the air was thick with the promise of rain.

Only a few dozen people turned up at the tiny hillside cemetery. Most of them were old, wrinkled veterans of the Resistance who'd fought with Boissier and Hawk in the dim, distant days of their youth.

A wind came up as they lowered the casket into the grave. It sent up a cloud of dust from the mound of fresh-turned earth and the priest's high-pitched lament was drowned out by its wailing.

When the brief service was over, the mourners slipped away one by one until only Hawk and myself were left.

"Sir," I said putting my hand on his arm, "I think we'd better head back to the city. It's going to start pouring any second now."

"Why don't you take the car," Hawk said quietly. "I'm going to stay here awhile and I'd like to be alone. Don't worry, Nick, I'll catch a taxi and meet you back at the hotel."

I walked back to the car where Lauren was waiting for me as the first drops of rain began to fall.

**DON'T MISS THE NEXT NEW
NICK CARTER SPY THRILLER**

CHESSMASTER

"How about a drink?" I asked Borga.

"I admit I can use one," he replied.

I went looking for a bottle and remembered that there had been one in Belnikov's room. I was in there when I heard a knock on the door. I heard Borga yell, "No, wait," and, hurrying to get back into the front room again, I saw Borga behind Boris, trying to keep him from opening the door, but to no avail. The door was open and I heard one shot. Borga pulled his gun as Boris was thrown back from the door, apparently from the force of the first shot. I heard a second shot and heard Borga shout out in pain as he was apparently hit. I had to hurdle over Boris to reach the door, and by the time I did there was no one there.

"Damn!" I shouted. I looked back, torn between chasing the assailant and checking to see if Borga was all right. He solved that dilemma for me by shouting, "Go ahead, go ahead!"

I jumped out into the hall, crouched low in case of gunfire. When there was none I had to decide which direction the assailant might have gone, up or down. From the position of the elevator, I was sure he hadn't gone in there, so I ran to the stairway, hoping I'd be able to hear him and determine whether he—or, if my theory was right, she—was going up or down.

I broke through the exit door, once again going low, with my gun out in front of me. I stopped to listen for footsteps and heard none. I took this to mean that the assailant had gone up to the roof. Had the assailant gone down, I'd still be able to hear footsteps. I didn't think he or she had entered at another floor, because the exit doors were locked from the staircase.

So, I made a decision and started up to the roof. If I was wrong, then maybe Borga's man downstairs would catch the shooter. If I was right, then Borga's other man and myself would have him or her trapped on the roof.

As I reached the door to the roof I heard an exchange of gunshots outside and knew I'd made the right decision. I went through the door and went into an immediate roll. I bumped into someone lying on the roof, and then realized that it was Borga's man. He was injured, but appeared to be alive.

It was dark on the roof with the only light of any kind coming from a just less-than-half moon. I stayed where I was, flat down on the roof, listening.

"You can't get off this roof," I shouted out.

There was no reply, but I could hear someone scurrying about, probably looking for some other way off the roof. I didn't know for sure that there wasn't some other way off, but I was hoping to make the shooter think so.

I took the opportunity to feel for a pulse in the downed man's neck, and I found one. It was fairly steady, and I told the guy he'd be okay, not knowing if he was even able to understand me. I patted him on the back and repeated that he'd be okay, hoping that at least my tone would relay the message to him.

I kept my gun out in front of me, although I would have preferred not to use it. My only chance of that, I thought, was to talk the assailant into surrendering.

"Give up," I called out, "you're outnumbered."

Through the darkness, as my eyes got used to it, I could make out some light stands around the roof, but the lights were not on. Presumably, they were controlled by some master switch, either inside the hotel, or out there on the roof. It would have been helpful if there were a switch on the roof, and if I could find it without being shot.

I was attempting to decide what my next move should be when very suddenly the rooftop was bathed in bright light as the lights on the light stands snapped on.

Both of us froze, and our eyes locked. I watched as the assailant, who apparently had been peering over the side of the roof at the time, stared back at me and almost directly into the light that was immediately behind me. As a matter of fact, he was facing right into the lights, while my back was to most of them. I saw him clearly as he was attempting to shade his eyes so he could fire his gun.

"Put the gun down," I shouted at him. I could see him clearly and could have fired at any time. I wanted to give him the opportunity to put down his gun, but he didn't seem inclined to do so. He kept shielding his eyes, holding the gun out in front of him, as if attempting to train it on me.

"Dammit, drop the gun now!" I shouted, getting up from the crouch I had been in. I kept my gun trained on him and he began to slide along the wall in an effort to escape the lights. I could see an opening in the wall where, presumably, there was a ladder that would lead from the roof down to wherever. If he attempted to go through that opening, onto the ladder, I'd have to fire.

That is, if he even was aware of the opening. If he wasn't, partially blinded as he was, he might just plunge through the opening accidentally, and fall anywhere from one to fifteen floors.

His back was against the wall as he continued along it, and I became convinced that he was simply trying to escape the glare of the lights, and was unaware of the danger of the opening.

"André, look out—" I shouted. He reacted to hearing his name and began to squeeze the trigger of his gun. I had no choice but to return fire. I fired twice, and both bullets struck him in the chest just as he reached the opening in the wall. He fell through the opening, and was gone.

—From CHESSMASTER
A new Nick Carter Spy Thriller
From Ace Charter in January